The Jessabelle House

The Coleman Series

Katie Winters

Chapter One

It was May 1— the last day of Samantha Coleman's marriage. Daniel had signed the divorce papers, and they now taunted her from the desk in her office. For twenty-five years, she'd been a woman who'd loved her husband with her body, soul, and mind. Yet here it was: proof that all the love in the world wasn't enough.

This was her worst nightmare. She was still too afraid to sign.

"Hey, boss. You got big plans this weekend?" Sharon had worked for Nantucket Recovery on the island for the past ten years, and she'd had a front-row seat to Samantha's heartbreak.

Samantha tugged the tie from her blond hair and felt it spill across her shoulders. She probably looked like a nervous wreck. "My daughters are meeting me for dinner tonight." They'd vowed to force her to sign the papers, bless them.

Sharon's smile brightened. "And how are Darcy and Rachelle doing? Gosh, it feels like yesterday they used to meet you here after school."

"I know! Where does the time go?" Samantha said sadly. "But Rachelle's semester in Boston is finished, and the two of them are living together this summer if you can believe it."

"That sounds like trouble," Sharon joked.

"I'm just grateful they've grown so close and want to share an apartment. I think it's pretty rare," Samantha admitted. This was such a contrast to her own siblings, who hardly spoke to her.

"My sister calls me once every six weeks to complain," Sharon said. "I wouldn't have wanted to live with her if she was the only roommate left in the world, God bless her soul."

Sharon disappeared into the lobby to speak to someone at the front desk. This left Samantha alone with the divorce papers. She scowled at them and checked the clock. It was five fifteen and nearly time for her to get out of there. Darcy had made dinner reservations for six thirty, and Samantha had promised to get there on time.

As though the universe itself was out to prove her wrong, her phone rang. As an addiction worker, Samantha knew better than to think her job stopped when the eight-hour day did.

"Hi, Kenny!" Samantha smiled as she answered. Kenny was one of her favorite clients. Over the years, he'd struggled tremendously with drug addiction but had shown promise since his return from rehab in January. She hoped it would stick this time.

"Ms. Coleman?" The voice was not Kenny's. A shiver of fear raced down Samantha's spine. "It's Connie. Kenny's girlfriend?"

"Of course. Hi. Is Kenny all right?" Samantha's veins

pumped with adrenaline. Already, she rushed for the coat rack to grab her spring jacket.

Connie's voice wavered. "He's locked himself in the bathroom. He can't stop crying. I don't know if he's using again, or if he's planning to use, or..."

"It's okay, Connie. Do you still live in the same place?" Samantha reached for her keys and flew out of the office, waving at Sharon as she passed her.

Connie and Kenny lived in a small apartment building on the outskirts of Nantucket's downtown. They were in their early thirties, worked in tourism, and hoped to buy a bigger place and have a family in the next few years. This was what Kenny had told Samantha when she'd last seen him. Still, Samantha knew addiction was the hardest thing to beat. It was a nasty disease, and she'd seen her fair share of it.

In the car, Samantha called her eldest daughter Darcy as she drove.

"I hope you aren't trying to get out of this dinner," Darcy answered.

Samantha's tone was stern. "I just have to check on a client. I'm not sure how long it will take."

Darcy didn't say anything. Both of Samantha's daughters knew how essential Samantha's career was. It was life-altering for her clients. Still, the immediacy of some of the situations often meant that Samantha put her friends and family second.

"I promise we'll do it today," Samantha said to Darcy. "I'll call you when I'm done, okay?"

"Okay. Good luck, Mom. Love you."

As Samantha told Darcy she loved her, she parked her car outside Kenny and Connie's apartment building, stopped the engine, and rushed to the second floor. Before she had time to knock, Connie opened the door. Her eyes were hollow and frightened.

"He's still in the bathroom," Connie said softly.

Behind the closed bathroom door, Kenny's sobs echoed. Although Samantha had many clients who relapsed, it was always heartbreaking— something she'd never get used to. This was compounded by the fact that she'd built strong relationships with many of them. She understood why they'd abused either alcohol or drugs in the first place, and she recognized the fear they carried with them every single day. More than that, she knew how important sobriety was for them. Oftentimes, they just couldn't manage it.

"Kenny? It's Sam." Samantha waited, listening as Kenny's sobs quieted for a moment. "Can you hear me?"

Kenny's voice was weak. "Yeah."

"Kenny, can you tell me what happened?" Samantha asked.

Kenny's cries escalated for a moment. Connie collapsed on the couch and put her face in her hands.

"I can't do this, Sam. I don't know how to do it."

"I know, Kenny. I know it's difficult." It took everything Samantha had not to show how sad she felt too. "Remember what we've talked about over the years? That you aren't alone in this. That you don't have to fight this by yourself."

"I don't know."

"You do know," Samantha urged. "I've been with you every step of the way. Connie's been here too. You don't have to fall back into this. Just because today happened doesn't mean all that progress is lost. You're stronger than this."

"I'm so angry at myself," Kenny muttered. It was almost too soft to hear.

"You have to set that aside, Kenny. You have to forgive yourself," Samantha whispered. "The only thing important in the world right now is getting you healthy again. Remember everything you told me last time you were in my office? That you want to have children with Connie? That you want them to be proud of who you are?"

Kenny's voice grew volatile again. "You just can't understand."

Samantha tilted her head. Addicts frequently said this, and perhaps it was mostly true. Addiction was a tricky thing to comprehend. Maybe, in some small way, Samantha had been addicted to the love of her husband; maybe she'd even been addicted to his cruelty. But neither of those things was a drug.

"I mean, come on! You're a Coleman!" Kenny cried. "You came from everything. You could never understand what it means to come from dirt."

Samantha bristled. Now that she'd been separated from her husband for two years, she'd officially gone back to her maiden name, Coleman. She hadn't expected these consequences.

"I know it might seem that way, Kenny," Samantha said, "but my father and I have hardly spoken in years. He genuinely hates my guts." She didn't add that her father, Roland Coleman, hadn't given her a cent since she'd moved out at eighteen.

Kenny moaned. Samantha's voice softened.

"Why don't you come out here? Connie's going to make some tea. Together, we can discuss a plan."

"Just like last time?" Kenny asked. He sounded defeated.

Samantha understood she had to try a different tactic. She bit down on her lower lip and considered his anger, his resentment toward people like the Colemans. How could she ensure he knew she wasn't the enemy?

"Kenny?"

"Yeah?"

"I can never understand what it's like to be you," she admitted. "Never, ever. I don't think anyone can."

Kenny remained silent. Samantha pressed on.

"You mentioned my family. As I said already, my father hates me— my siblings hardly speak to me, and for a long time, I was so lost."

"Why does your father hate you?" She could hear Kenny shuffle to a standing position, intrigued. She heard him unlock the door, but he kept it closed.

"As you said already, my family is and has always been a prestigious family on Nantucket," Samantha explained. "When I told my dad I wanted to go to university and complete my BA in social work, he flew off the handle."

"What?" Kenny was incredulous. This time, he opened the door just a crack. His eyes were bloodshot, and his face was very pale and slick with sweat.

"He told me if I went through with social work, he would no longer recognize me as his daughter," Samantha continued. Her voice was strong, even as she translated one of the greatest sorrows of her life.

Kenny opened the door a little bit wider. "But you help people."

Samantha shrugged. "The Colemans don't help people. They make money to pile on top of the money they already have. And social work doesn't exactly bring in heaps of gold."

Kenny's lips wavered. As he began to warm to her, he looked on the edge of a smile. *How could she draw him the rest of the way into the living room?* He needed water; he needed reason. *How could she get him to detox again? To take himself and his needs seriously again?* They'd done such tremendous work together, but the work was never over.

"I'm sure you'd like to tell your father a thing or two," Kenny said.

Samantha shivered. "There's so much I'd love to tell Roland Coleman that it isn't even funny. But I'd prefer to spend my free time with people like you. Good people who are doing their best in a cruel world." She locked eyes with him and added, "Good people who know that you have to choose who you are in this life rather than let society dictate it."

Kenny set his jaw. Bit by bit, the door opened wider to reveal the mess of the bathroom, which he'd torn apart. His hair was wild, unkept, and unwashed. But his breath came easier. With his hand on the wall, he steadied himself, then took a breath and stepped into the living room. Samantha stayed right by his side, ready to support him if he needed it.

It would be a terribly long road. But as Samantha watched Connie hug him and whisper sweet things to him as he shook with sorrow, she knew the road would be worth it.

And for the millionth time in her career, she was grateful she hadn't listened to Roland Coleman. She'd been born for this type of work, and no one would convince her otherwise. This was her world.

Chapter Two

Samantha pulled up outside the restaurant at eight-fifteen, almost two hours late. Through the window, she could see Darcy and Rachelle on either side of a table, sipping wine and eating appetizers. They could have been twins with their long and voluminous blond hair, sweet smiles, and easy laughter. Even now, as Samantha walked toward the front door, Darcy said something that made Rachelle burst out laughing.

When Samantha appeared at the table, her daughters leaped up to hug her.

"I'm sorry I'm late," Samantha said with a sigh. She collapsed into the chair beside Darcy and rubbed her temples.

"We get it, Mom," Rachelle replied. She nudged the bread bowl across the table. "Guessing you've hardly eaten today?"

"You guessed right." Samantha inhaled a piece of crispy baguette. "Oh, but Rachelle! It's so good to see you. You're back! Finally!"

Rachelle chuckled. "I was just here three weeks ago."

"But now you're back-back," Samantha affirmed. "How were finals?"

Rachelle went to culinary school in Boston. Since she'd been a girl, she'd been experimental in the kitchen, devoted to concocting delicious recipes for her father, mother, and sister. This experimentation had led her all the way to an estimable school, where she chopped, diced, sautéed, baked, and flambéed her way to the top of the culinary food chain. Samantha's real wish was for Rachelle to open a restaurant on Nantucket. There was certainly enough tourism to go around.

Rachelle described the six-course meal she had to cook for one of her professors. Apparently, the fourth course had nearly fallen apart in the skillet, and Samantha and Darcy listened with rapt attention as Rachelle described a cooking process neither of them understood.

The server arrived to take Samantha's wine order and all food orders. Together, they decided on a wide array of their favorites to share— salmon, a black bean quesadilla, and a burger with goat cheese.

"And onion rings," Samantha said.

"You only order onion rings when you really need them," Darcy pointed out. "Must have been a day for the books."

Rachelle's eyes widened. "And it's about to get even more interesting. Did you bring them?"

Samantha sighed. *Had it really come to this?* Just as the server returned with her glass of chardonnay, she heaved the stack of divorce papers onto the table and said, "Ta-da."

Rachelle and Darcy eyed the papers curiously. On the final page was their father's signature, one they'd all seen over and over again. This time, he'd used it to end their twenty-five-year marriage. It was surreal.

Just as quickly as she'd brought them out, Samantha returned the papers to her bag. "Let's not spoil dinner," she suggested, raising her glass of wine.

"Mom," Darcy and Rachelle groaned.

"Don't you want him off your back?" Rachelle asked timidly.

Samantha wasn't sure what she wanted. Everything she was currently supposed to want seemed to fight against everything she'd ever wanted before. When she'd met Daniel Earnheart at the age of eighteen, she'd been fresh off her rift with her father. Daniel had told her she was brave, strong, and confident. She could be whoever she wanted to be— and that meant not following in her father's footsteps. She'd fallen in love with Daniel almost immediately. They'd married when she was twenty and pregnant with Darcy. The rest was history.

"So, Darcy. How are things at the beauty clinic?" Samantha switched topics without subtlety.

Darcy rolled her eyes. "It's been so busy. People come in from all walks of life, wanting our services. It's very intimate."

"I would be terrified to give a Botox injection," Rachelle whispered. "What if you put it in the wrong place, and their face got all wonky?"

Darcy grimaced. "That's why you have to be a trained injector. It's never happened to me, but, of course, it happens. It's not always easy to understand how Botox will affect the muscle."

Samantha sipped her wine and remembered her first Botox injections. She'd been thirty-six and in the early stages of noticing just how cruel and manipulative Daniel had gotten. Her first assumption was that she'd gotten too old-looking for him, and she'd fled to a private beauty clinic and asked for an injection or two. Although she'd felt bright-eyed and youthful, Daniel's treatment of her had only worsened.

Their food finally arrived a few moments later. Samantha did her best to split everything into thirds, grateful for her daughters, who ate healthy foods and didn't starve themselves or hate their bodies. In Sam's profession, she'd seen so many addicts who struggled with body image and food. Even she, back in her teenage years, hadn't felt very good in her body. The Coleman image had been all-important. According to her father, it had been essential to show the Colemans to be the brightest, most prosperous, and most beautiful people on the island. This meant that things like "dessert" had flown out the window very early on in Samantha's life.

"Do you want dessert?" Samantha asked her daughters after they scraped their plates clean.

Rachelle and Darcy laughed and shook their heads.

"You're just trying to buy time," Darcy suggested.

Samantha waved at the server, who approached. "Can I get you anything else?"

"I'll have another glass of wine," Samantha said. "Girls? Another glass?"

Her daughters rolled their eyes and went along with it. Still, Samantha knew they were right. The divorce papers needed to be signed— it had gone on too long. Rachelle and Darcy had said tonight was the night. For the first time ever, Samantha had given them the reins. This, she'd told a friend, was a monumental moment in a mother's life— the moment you allowed your children a small bit of power over you.

After dinner, Samantha, Rachelle, and Darcy stepped into the chill of the evening. Just blocks away was the colonial home Samantha and Daniel had bought when the girls were very young. On instinct, they directed themselves toward it, chatting easily as they hurried into the warmth. It could have been any other night, except it wasn't. This was the last night they would spend in the old house together. The movers would come tomorrow at ten.

When they reached the colonial, Samantha, Rachelle, and Darcy stood out on the sidewalk and took in the last view of it. Stars sparkled in the inky black sky above, and in the distance, a dog howled into the night. For years, Samantha had assumed she and Daniel would grow old in that house. "We'll have to install a ramp for our wheelchairs," she'd joked to Daniel when they'd still been in love.

Turns out, she would walk out of the old colonial on her own two feet rather than a stretcher, like she'd planned.

Samantha had already taken the majority of the things she wanted to keep to storage. This left the rest of the house with a hodgepodge of strange, leftover things—furniture the movers would take to storage, furniture they would take to second-hand stores, and boxes labeled "miscellaneous" or "books." Rachelle and Darcy had already gone through their upstairs bedrooms to ensure they had all the treasures they wanted, which had been a tear-filled afternoon for Samantha.

Samantha turned on the light in the kitchen and put the kettle on the stovetop. Her daughters sat at the kitchen table, which would go to a second-hand store tomorrow.

"You'll be at the new apartment tomorrow?" Rachelle asked.

"That's the plan." Samantha was apprehensive about the little apartment she'd decided to rent. It was only a few blocks away, with a living room, a bedroom, a kitchenette, and a bathroom. It felt bizarre to move into a little apartment as though she had moved backward through time. She felt like she was eighteen years old again.

"We should have a housewarming!" Darcy said.

"I don't think there's much space for that," Samantha said. "Maybe I should get a cat and become a crazy old lady."

Darcy shot Sam a look. "Mom, you're forty-five. That's the new thirty."

"Is it? How does the science work on that?" Samantha joked.

"It's just that you have a lot of time," Rachelle affirmed. "You're young and vibrant. You have a killer career. There's probably a guy out there who would fit into your life perfectly."

Samantha's heart thudded. *How could she translate to her daughters how fearful she was of romance?* Daniel had promised to love and adore her. He'd promised "till death do us part." Yes, people got divorced all the time; she knew that. But Daniel hadn't just wanted a divorce. He'd built up to the divorce with insults that had had permanent damage to her psyche. When she'd gained a bit of weight over Christmas, he'd referred to her stomach as her "middle-aged belly." When clients of hers had relapsed, he'd suggested she hadn't done her job correctly.

More than that, when Samantha had finally broken down and asked him to stop being so cruel, he'd taken off. For over a week, she hadn't known where he was. She'd been listless and frightened. Because he'd broken her down so much, she hadn't known how to live her life without him. This was a common thing she saw in other people's relationships, especially in her line of work. It had taken years of reflection to understand she'd become the same.

When Daniel had returned, he'd confessed he'd been in New York City. There, he'd "finally" broken down and had an affair. Samantha had been too afraid to ask if it was the first affair he'd had.

Naturally, Daniel had fallen in love with this woman. *"But it wouldn't have ever happened if you wouldn't have pushed me away. I loved you, Samantha. So much."*

As Rachelle and Darcy sipped their tea in the kitchen for the very last time, Samantha remained at the counter. Her heart was in her throat.

"Can I ask something?"

Her daughters stopped talking and turned to look at her.

"You know that your dad and I's relationship wasn't exactly healthy, right?" Samantha's voice rasped. "I mean, you know that if a man treats you the way your father treated me, you shouldn't fall in love with him. Right?"

Darcy and Rachelle stood quickly and hurried to their mother. With their arms wrapped around her, they assured her how much they understood this. That since they could remember, their father hadn't been kind to their mother, and that they'd actually prayed for a divorce when they'd been younger.

Samantha's eyes filled with tears. "I hope it wasn't so bad for you to grow up with us."

"No!" Rachelle cried. "It wasn't. We loved both of you."

"We just knew something wasn't right," Darcy said. "And we wanted you to be happy."

Rachelle cupped her elbow. "He's gone. He started a new life. Isn't it time you allowed yourself a new life too?"

Samantha sighed. After a dramatic silence, she removed the divorce papers from her bag, along with a pen. The legal jargon was stiff as cement. As she signed her name, her daughters were very quiet. Samantha expected herself to feel something. She expected herself to picture Daniel on their wedding day, on their first date, or on the day Rachelle had been born. Instead, her mind was black.

When it was finished, Samantha told her daughters how much she loved them. Tensions were high, and everyone cried. Still, the hard part was over. It was time to move on.

Just as her daughters disappeared upstairs to sleep in their beds for the final time, Samantha's phone rang. It was her mother, Estelle.

"Hi, Mom." Samantha blinked back tears. "How are you?"

Estelle's voice was strained. "I'm sorry to call you so late, honey."

"Is everything okay?"

Estelle hesitated. "I hate to be the one to tell you this. We just got the news that Aunt Jessabelle passed away. I know how much you loved her."

Samantha stood in the shadows of her kitchen and closed her eyes. "My gosh," she said, feeling her heartbeat start to race. "I loved her so much." The pain in her chest tripled in size, and she found it hard to breathe.

Chapter Three

1995

I t was June 21, and time for another annual Coleman Solstice Party. Samantha Coleman was seventeen years old and the "odd duck" of the family, or so she'd overheard someone say. Perhaps this was true; if it was, should she care? She was sharp, witty, and very stubborn, and she didn't let anyone tell her what to do— not her father, nor her teachers, nor her brother, Charlie. As a girl, it had already become very clear to her that the world was "given" to men, and women were expected to help carry the load. This didn't work for her.

Samantha was the middle child of Roland and Estelle Coleman. Charlie was two years older than she was, and Hilary was two years younger. Already, Charlie and Hilary were golden Coleman children and planned to uphold the Coleman family image by supporting their father's real estate development business. Samantha couldn't imagine a worse fate.

Samantha had recently read a novel about a social worker who specialized in helping people with addictions. Although the addiction counselor in the novel had been a man, Samantha had seen herself in him. He fought for what was right. He understood the science of addiction and helped struggling people to the light on the other side. In such a dark and often tumultuous world, Samantha couldn't imagine a better way of living than helping people.

When Samantha had mentioned her dreams of social work to her mother, Estelle had winced and said, "Oh, honey, maybe you should talk to your father." Samantha hated when her mother said that. *Why did she have to field everything to her father? Why did he have eternal power over her life?*

On the afternoon of June 21, Estelle knocked on Samantha's door and handed over a plastic-wrapped party dress. Samantha removed the wrapping and stared at a ritzy dress that did not suit her style in the slightest.

"Mom, it looks like it's meant for old women," Samantha pointed out.

Estelle grimaced. "You know how important this party is to your father."

"I know. But does the importance of the party have anything to do with me dressing like I'm eighty-seven?"

"We can't have an incident like last time," Estelle said with a small smile.

Samantha laughed, remembering how she'd worn a pair of shorts and an oversized flannel to the last solstice party, trotting confidently through Roland's most esteemed clients and eating fancy food with her hands. She'd been grounded for weeks.

"Honey, I just don't want there to be any bad blood tonight," Estelle begged. "It's just a silly party. I know that. You know that. Can't you just wear the dress? Mingle a little bit? I promise you can go back to your room around eleven."

In the next room, fifteen-year-old Hilary played Janet Jackson songs on her tape deck. Two rooms over, Charlie and his buddy talked loudly about a beach party they'd been to recently.

"Are you making them wear something specific?"

Estelle grimaced and stepped away from Samantha's door. "Just promise you'll make an appearance at the party around six! Wear the dress, Sam. Tomorrow, the party will be just a memory. Let's make it a forgettable one, okay?"

Samantha returned to her bedroom and threw the dress on her bed. Its sequins caught the June sunlight and taunted her. Since she could remember, she'd detested the Coleman Solstice Party, and this dress only intensified that hatred. Always, she'd been off to the side of the crowd, watching her father mingle with "elites," his eyes as hungry for money as theirs.

A friend at Nantucket High had suggested Samantha just hated money because her family had always had it. Samantha had protested this, although she wasn't sure she was right. Money was a constant conversation topic in the Coleman family. It was the reason for life itself. She hadn't heard her father say "I love you" in many years, but he had informed her of stock and real estate hikes and the prices of approaching yachts. When Samantha had asked to get a job waitressing at a restaurant on the beach, her father had acted as though she wanted to jump off a cliff. "The Colemans can't be seen working a job like that. Don't you understand? Everything we do is under scrutiny."

It was hard for Samantha to accept that everything she did was a part of her father's brand.

Around six, Samantha met Hilary on the staircase. Hilary wore a simple white dress and a pair of heeled sandals, and her hair was shiny and clean. She eyed Samantha's dress and looked on the verge of making fun of it.

"Don't," Samantha warned.

"Uh-oh. The ice queen has come out to play." Charlie bounded down the staircase in a pair of shorts and a button-down. Nice fashion was so easy for men.

"Don't listen to him," Hilary tried. "Let's just have fun. Okay?" Her eyes begged Samantha to behave, just this once.

Already, over fifty people partied across the grounds of the Coleman estate. The grounds rolled evenly from the beautiful house and then opened out along the Nantucket Sound, which glistened with sunlight. In every respect, it was a ridiculous sight to see every single day of Samantha's life. Because she suspected she wouldn't have the money her father had later in life, she tried to be grateful for the view while she still had it.

The party was elaborate, as usual. Waiters breezed through Nantucket elite and served light hors d'oeuvres. Women in iconic dresses stood near the pool with champagne glasses, their faces bored. The few children who were there wore full suits and what looked like flower girl dresses. Samantha grabbed a mango juice from a passing waiter and tried to find her sister's eye. Already, Hilary had spotted a girlfriend and shot away from Samantha, who drank her juice alone.

Across the pool, Roland held court. Beside him, Estelle smiled easily and chatted with Roland's clients' wives. Although Samantha loved her mother to bits, Estelle's eagerness to please her father turned her stomach. *Didn't she see what a fake he was?* When Samantha mentioned this to Hilary, Hilary gasped and said, *"But you don't want them to get divorced, do you?"* She'd said it as though divorce was the worst thing that ever happened to people.

Behind her parents, Samantha spotted her saving grace. There, among a number of other Nantucket socialites, was Samantha's favorite person in the world: her great-aunt Jessabelle. She was fifty-five and absolutely iconic, with a sharp style, effervescent blond hair, which she still dyed, and remarkable wit. She'd never married or had children, and she was the head librarian at the downtown Nantucket Library, which thrilled Samantha to no end.

Samantha hurried around the pool and waited for her great-aunt Jessabelle's conversation to stall. When it did, Samantha leaped forward and hugged Jessabelle, who laughed at her energy.

"Where on earth have you been all week?" Jessabelle asked. "You were supposed to come around for another cribbage match."

"You've beat me the past five times! I'm nursing my wounds," Samantha said.

"I'll go easy on you." Jessabelle winked at her. She then lowered her voice and scanned the party. "Do you want to guess how many of these solstice parties I've been to over the years?"

"Are they always the same?" Samantha asked.

Jessabelle's eyes twinkled. "I can remember a few exciting ones."

"Ugh. You have to tell me," Samantha said. "It's hard for me to believe the Colemans were anything but boring stiffs."

Jessabelle laughed quietly just as Roland approached and touched her shoulder. "Aunt Jessabelle!" He hugged her. "I'm so glad you're here. I wanted to talk to you about something." All at once, Roland led Jessabelle away without bothering to say hello to Samantha. It was as if she hadn't been there at all.

Samantha grabbed a soda and wandered around the party, people-watching. Charlie flirted with a pretty girl whose dress was form-fitting and feminine, unlike Samantha's, which still seemed more appropriate for a retirement party. Hilary ate ice cream with a friend of the family and put her legs in the pool, and still avoided Samantha's eye. A little while later, a band arrived and began to play some light blues. Samantha decided the saxophonist was sort of cute, which kept her momentarily amused. He scrunched up his face during his solo, and the crowd roared with applause.

Samantha decided to go sit next to Hilary and put her legs in the pool, as well. She wouldn't force Hilary to speak to her, and she wouldn't invade her conversation. She just needed a place to go until she could head upstairs and hide. Estelle had said she could leave by eleven; Samantha was counting on it.

But before Samantha reached Hilary, the teenage son of one of Roland's clients approached. He was one of these rich, handsome, arrogant types— the ones who already knew the world would be gifted to them on a silver spoon.

"Tell me, Samantha." He raised his thick eyebrows provocatively. At first, Samantha thought he was flirting with her. "What the heck are you wearing?"

Samantha's nostrils flared. Anger became the only thing she understood. "What did you say?"

"I said, why did you raid your grandmother's closet before you came to the party?" His smile was enormous.

Samantha hated him. She wasn't even sure what his name was. "Since we're being so open about our feelings, can I ask you a question?"

"Of course."

"Why did you have your bottom sewed over your face? Was it really that bad before the surgery?"

The guy's jaw dropped with rage. He wasn't accustomed to people talking to him like that. "If you weren't a Coleman, people would walk all over you, you know," he told her sharply. "We would rip you apart."

And suddenly, because her rage was insurmountable, Samantha pressed her hands against the guy's chest and shoved him into the pool. He splashed into the turquoise water and went under. In his wake, water splattered across expensive evening gowns and suits that had been handcrafted in Italy. Samantha didn't care. She relished his face as he popped out of the pool to hurl insults at her.

Already, a hand was around her arm. As she was tugged into the house, she laughed outrageously as though she'd gone crazy. In the downstairs hallway, her father turned her around, grabbed her shoulders angrily, and began to scream at her. He was so close to her ears that she could hardly make out what he said. Fright overtook her, so much so that she got her emotions mixed up and nearly smiled.

When her father released her, he pointed at the staircase and told her to go to her room immediately. Samantha fled as if her life depended on it. When she reached the next floor, however, she found Aunt Jessabelle in the shadows. Her face was etched with worry.

"Let's go for a drive," she said. Her keys jangled in her hand.

"I have to go to my room," Samantha said simply.

"He'll never know," Jessabelle reminded her.

Samantha knew she was right. Roland would be working the crowd the rest of the night.

Jessabelle drove a white convertible with leather seats. Like everyone else in her family, she had money— but the money had been passed down from her own father, who'd died a very long time ago and left his two daughters very comfortable. As Samantha buckled her seat belt, Jessabelle searched for a good song on the radio and finally decided on Dido. Unlike other women around her age, she liked to keep up with the going trends in pop culture. It was remarkable.

For a little while, they drove without speaking. It was as though Jessabelle could sense how frantic Samantha felt.

"He just made me so mad, Aunt Jessabelle," Samantha said finally. She punched her leg. "I couldn't just let him get away with it."

Jessabelle smiled gently. Her hair rushed out behind her as the car careened across the island.

"And I feel like I don't belong in that family!" Samantha cried. "Dad hates me. Mom's constantly scared that I'll make Dad angry. And Charlie and Hilary seem unbothered by everything that happens in this crazy family."

Jessabelle shrugged. "You don't have to be like your family, you know. It's up to you to decide who you want to become. You've been given an extraordinary position in life, but that doesn't mean you have to keep it or follow the same path."

Samantha was quiet for a bit. It had never fully occurred to her that one day, she could remove herself from the parts of her life she didn't like.

"You're still young," Aunt Jessabelle pointed out. "But all that will change next year when you go to college. You'll be given time and space to think about who you are and who you want to be. And that is the greatest gift of all."

"I know Dad won't like what I want to become," Samantha said quietly.

"That's his problem. Not yours." Aunt Jessabelle's eyes flashed. After a pause, she added, "I don't want you to get the wrong idea. I adore my sister's children. Roland and Grant are my blood. But that doesn't mean I have to agree with them, either."

Samantha nodded. In the distance, the Coleman Solstice Party had begun to release fireworks, and they exploded over the Nantucket Sound in extravagant colors.

"My sister and I used to have the best time at those silly parties," Aunt Jessabelle said wistfully. "I can't believe she's been gone so many years."

"Grandma Margaret was wonderful," Samantha agreed. "But you two were different, weren't you?"

"Very different," Jessabelle affirmed. "But we had each other's backs through everything. With her gone, I've felt less connected from the world, as though she was the last tether I had to the ground." After a pause, she added, "Although I have to admit, having you around lately has reassured me."

"Am I a little like Grandma Margaret?" Samantha asked. Her grandmother had died at the young age of fifty-one, and her memories of the older woman weren't complete or nuanced.

Jessabelle laughed. "I don't know. I think you're a little like both your grandmother and I, but you're also completely yourself. Stay true to that. You promise me?"

Samantha promised. She then reached across the convertible and squeezed her great-aunt's hand. Over the years, Jessabelle had lost so much, but she remained a powerful and strong individual, one Samantha was honored to know.

Chapter Four

Present Day

I t was hard for Samantha not to picture Daniel's new apartment in New York City, especially now that she had her own. Although she hadn't seen photographs, she knew he lived in a high-rise apartment building with a doorman and ornate furnishings, that he had a state-of-the-art kitchen, and that his girlfriend was a full eleven years younger than Samantha was— all things that made Samantha's imagination go wild.

Daniel's girlfriend's age shouldn't have bothered Samantha. In some ways, it didn't. Age was just a number, and Daniel's new girlfriend was a consenting adult. Then again, she probably hadn't had to google "Botox" or "retinol" yet. She hadn't given birth. Her body hadn't gone through what Samantha's had. She was his shiny new toy.

What happened when the girlfriend wasn't so new

anymore? Would Daniel go out and get a fresh one? Was that the type of guy he was? Was that really the man Samantha had decided to have babies with?

"You cannot be hard on yourself. People change. Maybe Daniel changed more than most people." Estelle, Samantha's mother, sat at the kitchen table in the new apartment. She was already dressed for Jessabelle's funeral, and she looked regal. The milky pearls around her neck caught the light.

Samantha poured them both mugs of coffee and sat across from her. For the funeral, she wore a simple black dress without the sophistication of Estelle's. In many people's eyes, Samantha was no longer a Coleman, which meant she wasn't expected to dress like one. This was still a welcome relief, even so many years after her father had basically disowned her.

"Dad must have had a field day when he learned Daniel left me," Samantha said.

Estelle raised her eyebrows but didn't comment. Samantha knew better than to bring her father up in conversation. She was just grateful for her constant connection with her mother, who'd struggled with Samantha's choices but ultimately respected her. When Samantha had fully stepped away from her father and carved her own path, Estelle had told her she would love her forever, no matter what.

Of course, when Samantha had had her daughters, Estelle hadn't stood a chance. She'd stopped by Samantha and Daniel's place nearly every day to hold the babies and help Samantha around the house. When Samantha had asked Estelle if she told Roland about their times together, Estelle had said, "What Roland doesn't know won't hurt him."

It had hurt Samantha that her father hadn't taken the time or had any interest in getting to know her daughters, but she'd found a way to shove that pain down.

Not long after Estelle arrived, Darcy and Rachelle came in. They hugged their grandmother and chatted as Samantha hurried into her bedroom to finish her makeup and hair. Five minutes in, there was a knock at the door, and Rachelle hurried to answer it.

"Mom! It's flowers!" she called.

"What?" Samantha laughed at her reflection in the mirror. When she entered the living room, she found Rachelle with a big bouquet. "Nobody has sent me flowers in like fifteen years."

But sure enough, her name was written on the little red card. Samantha tore it open and removed the note.

"It's from Daniel," she said, surprised.

"Oh. He must have heard about Aunt Jessabelle," Estelle said.

But Samantha shook her head. Instead, the notecard read simply: "Thanks for signing the divorce papers. Good luck on your next adventure." The words rattled her. Before she knew what she'd done, she shoved the flowers in the trash can. When she turned back, her daughters and mother gaped at her. None of them were stupid enough to ask her what she was doing.

Outside the apartment building, Estelle hugged Samantha and closed her eyes. "I think it's a fine little apartment. Remember, it's not forever."

But Samantha wasn't so sure. She had no plan beyond that week. She was forty-five, newly divorced, and a social worker with a subpar income.

"Love you," Samantha said. Together, she and her daughters waved to Estelle as she got into her car and drove off. At the funeral home, Sam knew Estelle would be glued to Roland's side, and Samantha and her children would just give them courtesy nods. It just made it easier on everyone.

In the car, Samantha said, "We can play a game up at the funeral home if you want."

Rachelle and Darcy eyed her curiously. "What are you talking about?" Darcy demanded.

Samantha smiled secretly. "You know your great-great-aunt Jessabelle was never married, right?"

"Yes," the girls answered in unison.

"But did you also know that she was just about the most romantic person in the world?" Samantha continued. "Over the years, I knew her to have many, many lovers. She broke hearts left and right because she refused to marry them."

Darcy and Rachelle chuckled with surprise.

"What's the game?" Rachelle asked.

"Well, let's see how many of her lovers we can count at the funeral!" Samantha suggested. "I imagine they'll all be between sixty and eighty years old, handsome, and very, very sad."

"In their sixties? So, Jessabelle dated men twenty years younger than her?" Rachelle asked, her eyebrow cocked.

"She told me later in life that men her age couldn't keep up with her," Samantha said.

"Maybe you should date a younger man, Mom," Darcy suggested.

Samantha's stomach curled. "Ugh. You couldn't pay me to date a twenty-something."

Both Darcy and Rachelle burst out laughing. Over the years, they'd shared many stories from their romantic lives, which was a remarkable thing for Samantha, as she'd had to be so secretive during her teenage years. It was only in the past twenty years that she and Estelle had opened up to one another, with the caveat that they wouldn't speak of Roland.

Jessabelle had been eighty-seven when she died. Frequently, she'd joked that all her friends had already died, but according to the enormous turn-out at the funeral home, this was not so. Samantha, Darcy, and Rachelle walked through the crowd and headed toward the front of the funeral home, where Aunt Jessabelle lay in her coffin with her hands folded gently over her stomach. Her beautiful blond hair glistened against the pillow, and her face was serene. It was bizarre to see her like this, of course. Normally, her face was scrunched with laughter or wide-eyed with excitement. But this was the final time Samantha would ever see that face— and she wanted to remember every crease and every fold and every strand of hair.

"She's so beautiful," Darcy remarked.

"She always was," Rachelle agreed. "With killer style till the end."

For a little while, Samantha, Rachelle, and Darcy sat in the second row of seats and watched as other mourners approached the casket. True to what Samantha had said, several of them could have been ex-lovers. They came alone and dabbed handkerchiefs beneath their eyes. When Samantha stood to ask one of them how they'd known her great-aunt, he got misty-eyed and said, "She was a treasure of a woman. I haven't seen her in ten years or so, but I've thought of her every day since." That was all he wanted to share.

"He's still in love with her," Rachelle whispered, impressed.

"That's the kind of legacy I want to leave behind," Darcy said.

Samantha smiled sadly. Her heart was some parts heavy, other parts light. Her great-aunt hadn't been herself in many years. Her memory had faded, and she'd required in-home care. In some ways, her death had freed her from the cage of her body. Still, Samantha ached for all the memories with Jessabelle she couldn't return to.

"You know, she was basically my grandmother," she said softly to her daughters. "I went over to her house all the time to play cards and bake cookies."

Rachelle and Darcy nodded. They'd heard this over and over again.

"Why do you think she never wanted to get married?" Darcy asked as another solo man approached the casket.

Samantha was fresh off her divorce and could totally understand why. But did she want to share such nihilism with her daughters? *Now was not the time.*

"I think she just wanted to be free without being tied down," Samantha reasoned. "Back in those days, women weren't treated equally. Women couldn't even open their own bank account until the sixties, for heaven's sake."

"That would never have worked for Aunt Jessabelle," Darcy agreed. "Sounds like she dodged a bullet."

Very soon after, the service began. A minister Samantha didn't recognize read a few scriptures and made a small speech about our time on earth and how it must inevitably come to an end. It wasn't an emotional service, but Samantha decided that was okay. Jessabelle would have wanted everyone to head home and drink wine in her honor, anyway.

When the funeral finished, Samantha stood, turned on her heel, and immediately locked eyes with her father, who stood with Estelle, Hilary, and Charlie on the other side of the room. Samantha's heartbeat sped up. She ripped her gaze away and turned to speak to her daughters, who asked if she was all right.

"Let's go somewhere after the burial," Samantha suggested. "I don't want to go back to that depressing apartment."

"It's not so bad!" her daughters spoke in unison again.

Samantha grimaced. "We can't go back there." For some reason, she'd begun to equate Jessabelle's burial plot with her drab divorcée apartment.

But as she spoke, her daughters' faces paled. Their eyes were focused on something behind Samantha, and Samantha shivered with fear. When she turned back, she found Roland in the center of the aisle. He continued to peer at her with a mix of nerves and animosity. As usual, he wore an immaculate suit, as it was essential to be seen looking excellent if you were a Coleman, even at your aunt's funeral.

"Dad." Samantha's voice was firm.

"Samantha." He raised his eyebrows.

Samantha wanted to tell her father she didn't have time for pleasantries. Then again, the one thing Jessabelle wouldn't have wanted was for Samantha to pick a fight with her father at her funeral.

"Do you have a minute?" Roland asked.

Samantha shrugged and followed her father to the far corner. She felt like a teenager and prepared herself for a full onslaught of insults. For not the first time, she wondered if, in marrying Daniel, she'd just married her father. Women did that. She just hadn't thought she was that kind of woman. The joke was on her, she supposed.

"I've just been to see the executor of Jessabelle's estate." Roland didn't pause for pleasantries.

"Oh." Samantha didn't smile.

"As you know, she was a philanthropist and donated the majority of her father's money to various charities," Roland continued. He said it as though it was the stupidest thing she'd ever done. "But she made a surprise addition to her will in recent years."

"Okay?" Samantha did not like talking to her father.

"It seems she's left you the Jessabelle House," Roland said simply.

Samantha's eyes widened. "What?" She was genuinely shocked. "Me?"

Roland shrugged as though he was just as confused as she was. "The executor will be in contact with you shortly. As far as I can tell, you have only to pick up the keys and sign a bit of paperwork. After that, the house is yours."

Samantha was flabbergasted. "Thank you for letting me know."

Roland nodded. His gaze was pointed toward the casket. The funeral director had begun to close it, sealing Jessabelle in forever. Samantha watched as well, captivated. Her heart burned with love for Jessabelle.

"I suppose we'll see you at the cemetery," Roland said stiffly. He then marched around Samantha and headed back to Estelle, who bobbed her head.

Samantha remained frozen in the corner. In her wildest dreams, she never imagined owning the Jessabelle House. Her little divorcée apartment could have been a closet there in comparison.

Darcy and Rachelle hurried over, both bug-eyed. It was a rare thing to witness their grandfather and their mother in conversation.

"What happened? What did he say, Mom?" Rachelle demanded.

Samantha stuttered.

"Mom? Are you okay?" Darcy asked.

"Jessabelle was always so good to me," Samantha whispered, feeling the tears well in her eyes. "But this takes the cake."

Chapter Five

I t had been a week since the funeral. Against all odds, time had marched forward, and it was now very nearly the middle of May. Rachelle had started her summer job at a restaurant called the Cru in the Nantucket Historic District, where she worked under a renowned chef who, it was said, could often be very hard on his staff. "But that's how you get really good, Mom. Someone has to push you," Rachelle explained. Darcy continued to fight the good fight at the beauty parlor while Samantha pushed herself through difficult days as a social worker.

The executor of the estate had said the keys to the Jessabelle House would be ready for Samantha soon—and in the meantime, the walls of the apartment threatened to close in on her. Her dreams were nothing but nightmares of how happy Daniel was. Gosh, she couldn't be more grateful to inherit the Jessabelle House. She needed it so badly.

On the morning she could pick up the keys, Samantha was in Boston to visit Kenny in rehab. In the ten days since he'd arrived, color had returned to his cheeks. His eyes were brighter. Although he still seemed sullen, he spoke with more optimism about the life he wanted to build with Connie. As Samantha drove away from the clinic, waves of worry for Kenny and his future crashed over her. He wanted desperately to get better, but Samantha knew this world through and through. The odds got worse every time her patients relapsed.

Still, she had to try. If Kenny was willing to, she had to be too.

Samantha returned to Nantucket by two p.m. and shivered with hunger. Sharon at the front desk demanded they head out to get some lunch. Very soon, they sat outside a coffee shop with sandwiches and coffees as the sun shone from the heavens. They talked about simple things, like the cockroach problem Samantha had in her apartment and Sharon's daughter's obsession with stuffed animals.

"Oh gosh. Keep your daughter that young!" Samantha cried. "What I wouldn't give to have one day with Rachelle and Darcy when they were that little."

Sharon laughed. "She drives me up the wall, sometimes."

"You'll forget all about that when she's in her twenties," Samantha affirmed.

Samantha briefly mentioned the finalization of her divorce, which piqued Sharon's curiosity. Ordinarily, Samantha wasn't so keen to talk about Daniel and everything that had gone wrong. There was no doubt the people at work had noticed how sad she'd been over the past several years, though.

"What now?" Sharon asked, her eyes alight.

"What do you mean? I'm divorced. I'm forty-five."

"Yes. But that doesn't mean you shouldn't put yourself out there. I mean, come on. Things between you and Daniel were over for quite a while, right?" Sharon asked.

Samantha scrunched her nose and took a bite of her sandwich.

"Here. Have you looked at the apps?" Sharon removed her phone from her purse and showed Samantha her dating profile. For as long as Samantha had known Sharon, she'd been single. Apparently, the father of her daughter had never been a part of their lives.

"There are so many of them," Samantha said. Sharon swiped through accountants, architects, gas station attendants, and stockbrokers.

"You can say what age you're looking for," Sharon said. "I put mine between thirty-eight and forty-eight."

"Is forty-nine too old for you?" Samantha teased. She thought it was silly.

"Don't laugh," Sharon said. "You would have fun if you went out with someone. Why not give yourself that gift?"

Samantha chewed her sandwich. She felt crippled with the truth: that she'd never loved anyone but Daniel. She'd never planned to. Besides, she was already a completely molded person with her own desires, dreams, and opinions. *What if whoever she dated next didn't like who she was?* Then again, Daniel hadn't even liked who she was. *Where did that leave her?*

"What about this guy?" Sharon suggested, showing a profile of a guy with a mullet and eighties sunglasses.

"Um, Sharon? Are you trying to kill me?" Samantha cackled.

"Maybe he could help you broaden your fashion sense," Sharon teased.

* * *

Samantha made it to the lawyer's office five minutes before closing. Jessabelle's executor was a handsome and charming man in his fifties, who explained he'd "adored" Jessabelle to pieces and had been very sorry to hear of her passing.

"I know she wasn't the same Jessabelle the past few years," he said. "But she was still a barrel of laughs. When she came in to adjust her will and give the Jessabelle House to you, she said she would give anything to see your expression when you found out."

Samantha's smile nearly broke her face. "Oh no. I'm going to cry!"

The lawyer chuckled and handed her a manila envelope in which he'd placed the keys. Afterward, she signed a few pieces of paperwork with ease, having practiced with divorce papers, and bid the lawyer goodbye. "I haven't been out to the Jessabelle House in such a long time," she said. "I'm guessing it's not in the best shape."

"Sounds like you've got a summer project on your hands."

In the car, Samantha called Rachelle excitedly to ask if she wanted to head out to the Jessabelle House. Darcy was in the room with her, and both squealed with excitement. "I'll be there in five," Samantha said.

Rachelle and Darcy burst into the car and chatted excitedly about Samantha's new "palace." Jessabelle hadn't resided in the old house in probably two years or so, but that meant that Rachelle and Darcy had many marvelous memories there— racing through the grounds, hiding in the nooks and crannies, and swimming in the ocean. Jessabelle had adored them. "*You are a wonderful* mother, Samantha," Jessabelle had said. *"I was never meant to be one, but you absolutely were."* When Samantha had asked Jessabelle why she'd never wanted children, Jessabelle laughed and said, *"I like my time alone."*

Before they drove out to the Jessabelle House, they stopped at a local grocery to grab wine and snacks for a light picnic on the veranda. Jessabelle wouldn't have wanted it any other way.

Together, Samantha, Darcy, and Rachelle breezed through the aisles. The girls chatted and giggled, throwing chips and fruit into the basket. Samantha led the way, pausing momentarily at the cheese counter. After she placed the Camembert in the basket, she turned abruptly and staggered into a woman coming the opposite way.

Her heart nearly burst. "Hilary?"

Hilary, Samantha's little sister, grinned nervously. She carried a basket laden with fruits and vegetables. "Hi, Sam." She glanced back at the girls and waved. "Hi, Rachelle. Hi, Darcy."

As usual with Hilary, things were strained. "How are things?" Samantha asked.

"Things are fine. No change." Hilary smiled meekly.

"And Ava?" Ava was Hilary's only child. She was twenty-one.

"She's good," Hilary replied with a shrug. After a pause, she added, "I was sorry to hear about Daniel."

"Oh. Yeah." Samantha's heart dropped. "It's been an adjustment."

They spoke like strangers, not like sisters. Samantha hated it but had no idea how to change it. When Roland deemed Samantha the black sheep of the family for not following in their footsteps, Hilary and Charlie had just gone along with it. It was as though they'd always suspected Samantha just didn't fit in, just as she had.

"Anyway, we're off to the Jessabelle House," Samantha explained.

"Right." Hilary's smile fell. "Congratulations."

Samantha nodded and edged away. "Have a good day." She then fled for the cash register, where she paid for their items, and hurried out the door. Her daughters ran to keep up with her. When they reached the car, they gasped and said, "What was that about?" But Samantha wasn't sure. She just hated the way her family looked at her— as though she was a stray dog.

Samantha drove them toward Siasconset as a gorgeous sunset dappled over the ocean. As they got closer, she allowed herself to get excited, really excited. The house was extraordinary. And it was hers! Nobody, not her father nor Hilary, nor Charlie, could take it away from her.

The Jessabelle House was situated on sprawling and glorious grounds just outside the charming village of Siasconset. From its extravagant veranda, you could see immaculate views of the Atlantic and Sconset Dunes, which, to Samantha, beat the views at her parents' place by a landslide. The house itself had a remarkable history, as it was designed by Charles H. Robinson, the architect credited with bringing Victorian architecture to the island, and it was previously used as a guest house and dining club, presumably before Samantha's great-grandfather had purchased it.

To up the drama, Samantha drove slowly down the long driveway. Bit by bit, the Jessabelle House came into view, standing proudly upon the bluff. Although Jessabelle had always called it a cottage, the four-bedroom, two-bath home would have sold for upward of five million. When Darcy had asked Samantha if she planned to sell, Samantha had said, *"Absolutely not."* She now pictured herself as a little old lady out on that veranda, with the Atlantic winds in her hair— just as Jessabelle had been.

Samantha parked the car outside the house. The three of them stepped out and gazed up at the gorgeous home, which, this close up, was admittedly quite rough around the edges. Shutters needed to be repaired; winds and rain had weathered portions of the veranda, and every bit of it needed a paint job. There was no telling what the inside looked like.

Still, it was all Samantha's.

Samantha used the keys to enter the front door. As she opened it, her nose filled with dust, and she sneezed. Darcy and Rachelle followed suit, and the three of them cackled.

"Oh boy. You can sure tell it hasn't been lived in for a few years," Rachelle commented as she looked around the room.

Downstairs, the living room furniture had been covered with white sheets. A grandfather clock gave the wrong time, and a painting on the wall was so heavy with dust that you couldn't make out what the image was supposed to be.

Samantha stepped further into the house, through the kitchen, where an animal had clawed through some of the cabinets, and through the dining room, where a window had a hole in it.

Upstairs, the bedrooms and bathrooms were in similar states of disarray. Samantha laughed to herself. "I'm guessing the three of us can't take on a project like this ourselves. I'll need to hire someone to give it a little TLC."

Rachelle winced. "What are you going to do?" She was referring to the money required for such a big project.

But Samantha was in luck. "We just sold the house, so I have a bit of money to play around with. Plus, I don't have to pay rent much longer. Lucky me." She chuckled.

Samantha fluttered a blanket across the veranda, and the three of them sat on it and watched the sky bleed with oranges, reds, and pinks. Samantha popped the cork from the bottle of wine as her daughters removed the snacks from the grocery bags. Years ago, she'd thought being a single parent would have been the loneliest and most terrifying thing in the world. Yet here she was, alone with her daughters. It was a dream.

"What do you think we should do with this place?" Samantha sipped her wine and eyed her daughters.

"You should give yourself a huge bathtub," Rachelle suggested.

"Oh. And you should put in the countertops you always wanted!" Darcy said.

Samantha cringed. *Had her daughters heard her arguing with Daniel about countertops? What a ridiculous fight that had been.*

Rachelle placed her head on her mother's shoulder. "We just want you to be happy, Mom. You know that, right?"

"I feel the same about you two," Samantha said.

A seagull cawed overhead. They lifted their eyes to watch as it streamed toward the sea.

"I hope you're ready for the cleaning event of your lives," Samantha joked after a little while.

Rachelle groaned. She was the less organized of the

two and had always had a messier bedroom. Darcy clapped.

"This is going to be so fun, Rachelle! You know how much I love to dust," Darcy said.

"She's so lame, Mom. How do you stand it?" Rachelle teased.

"Listen, Rachelle, we need that energy right now," Samantha said. "I'm not the biggest fan of cleaning, either. But this place needs some help, and we're the only ones around to give it."

Chapter Six

Unfortunately, it wasn't rare to encounter people with addictions on the island. The disease was in no way prejudiced; it loved every age, race, and background. In fact, it often worked its way into well-off families who, on paper, had done everything right.

Drug dealers managed to get their hands in every scene— and they were especially keen to get affluent teenagers hooked. They always had money, they had time, and often, their parents were too distracted with their vibrant social lives to pay attention until it was too late.

A few afternoons after Samantha got the keys to the Jessabelle House, she spoke with two sophisticated Nantucket parents about their teenager, Kathy, who Samantha had recently helped get into a private rehab facility not far from Hyannis Port on the mainland. Samantha sat in their luxurious living room on a couch that had probably cost twenty-thousand dollars, trying not to think about her own upbringing and the suffocation she'd felt as a Coleman.

Kathy's mother, a woman named Winona, was sleek and toned from hours of morning Pilates. She passed Samantha a mug of tea and did not look at her husband, Jeff, who sat in a suit and tugged at his collar sporadically. Kathy was their only daughter, and photographs of her in happier days hung on the walls. But if Samantha understood the dynamic correctly, she knew that Winona and Jeff had only paid attention to Kathy when she presented herself appropriately and was worthy of their attention. Addiction was a stain on their reputation.

Samantha spoke to Winona and Jeff about the rehab center and tried to prepare them for life post-rehab. She tried to instill in them that Kathy would need their attention and love more than ever after she came home. Winona and Jeff appeared to be attentive, but Sam saw otherwise. Only when Samantha mentioned that other teenagers in the community had addiction issues and that Kathy's addiction didn't exist in a vacuum did Winona speak.

"Are you suggesting that other students at school manipulated her into this?" she demanded. "Because I had been thinking about this. She mentioned people we don't know. People from questionable families."

Samantha's stomach twisted. "Right now, we can't point a finger. We can only build a nurturing world for Kathy. We can only remind her just how worthwhile it is to be alive— and sober."

Samantha left Kathy's estate with a bad taste in her mouth. As she backed out of their driveway, she twisted her head to ensure she didn't see her parents' place. It was only four houses down, a domineering white Victorian. It was the origin of her nightmares.

By the time Samantha reached the Jessabelle House,

the construction crew she'd called, Elrod and Sons, had arrived. They were three brothers, Derek, Patrick, and Brent, and they stood leaning against their business van with their chins lifted to take in the May light. It was impossible not to mention how handsome each of them was. They were in their mid-forties, with dark locks that were sprinkled with salt and pepper and crow's feet that showed a lifetime of laughter.

"Sorry I'm late!" Samantha called as she walked toward them.

"We're early," Derek corrected. He was a little bit taller than the others, the eldest, and his voice was deep and comforting. "We just wanted to have a picnic before we got started."

"A good old-fashioned picnic? What did you pack?"

Patrick chuckled and showed off the remains of what they'd packed: fruit, nuts, ham and cheese sandwiches, and sour cream and onion chips.

"Our mother always packed us lunches before she died," Brent said, blushing. "For a few years after she died, we got take-out."

"But it made us feel so empty," Derek affirmed.

Samantha's heart lifted. It was impossibly endearing that these forty-something men packed lunches for themselves and ate together the way they had as boys.

Patrick put the picnic basket in the van, and the three men followed Samantha up the steps to the veranda. From there, they could see Darcy and Rachelle through the open window, where they continued to clean with handkerchiefs around their hair. Their old t-shirts and jeans were already dirty. A speaker they'd placed inside played pop songs that echoed through the hallways.

"Hi, girls!" Samantha called. "How's it going today?"

Darcy and Rachelle wagged dust rags back.

"I see someone finally decided to join us?" Rachelle teased.

"We've been slaving away for hours," Darcy complained jokingly.

Samantha introduced Derek, Patrick, and Brent to her daughters. They waved timidly. Samantha then turned and asked Derek where they'd decided to start on the refurbishment. Just yesterday, she'd given them an extensive walk-through of the Jessabelle House, during which they'd discussed how she envisioned the space. The Elrod Brothers had given their professional opinions, and Samantha's excitement had mounted. There was so little she knew about construction work and refurbishment. When she'd told them this, Derek had said, "This was our father's business before ours. We grew up knowing how to enter a space and imagine it differently."

"It's a blessing and a curse," Patrick had joked.

Now, Derek said they'd decided one of them would work on the downstairs kitchen, another in the bathroom, and another on the walls of the downstairs living room.

"It isn't going to be an all-summer project," he explained. "The bones of the house are good. If anything, it just needs a coat of lipstick and some personal touches to make it yours. Based on your imagination for the place, coupled with the ideas we discussed yesterday, I think we can have it finished in a little more than a month."

"Better give us six weeks," Patrick quipped.

"Yeah, Derek. Don't overpromise. That was Dad's first rule," Brent said with a laugh.

Samantha waved. "Take all the time in the world you need. I'd love to enjoy the house sometime this summer, of course. But I guess we'll all be here together quite a bit, eating picnics on the veranda."

* * *

The very next day after work, she drove out to the Jessabelle House with food and beers, excited to see how far they'd gotten. But as it was still early-on in the project, she discovered they'd mostly torn things apart.

Samantha giggled as she entered the kitchen. Her nostrils filled with wood shavings and the smell of plaster. "I thought I asked you to build the place back up, not tear it down."

Derek popped up from behind the kitchen island and chuckled. His eyes glistened. "You know what they say. Out with the bad to make space for the good."

"That's what my friend said about my divorce," Samantha said. She'd reached the phase of trying to joke about Daniel, but it wasn't working.

But Derek took the joke in stride. He winced and said, "I know my way around refurbishing a house. But personal relationships? Leave that to the therapists."

"Technically, I'm a social worker," Samantha said. "You'd think I'd know my way around personal relationships more than I do."

"Uh-oh. Are you suggesting nobody really knows how anything works?" Derek feigned shock.

Samantha chuckled. Derek looked at her in a way she rather liked— a way that made her feel a little bit younger than her forty-five years. Or, not younger, exactly. More vibrant. More optimistic. More flirtatious.

Patrick popped into the kitchen to say hello. In the bathroom, Brent continued to tear something apart. A

speaker in the large, empty room played Bruce Spring-
steen, and the windows that remained in their panes
rattled.

Soon after, Darcy and Rachelle stopped by to say
hello and see what they could do to help. Rachelle had to
work the dinner shift that night and was jittery. "We have
a full night of reservations, and the chef is panicked. He
doesn't think we're ready."

To this, Darcy raised her eyebrow and said, "You all
know how to cook, right? What's the big deal?"

But Rachelle shook her head and gazed out at the
blue horizon.

Darcy told a story about a facial gone wrong at the
beauty parlor that afternoon. "She started screaming and
saying her face was burning. I immediately washed her
face and tried to calm her down. But when I tried the
same solution on my own skin, there was nothing wrong
with it! It was weird, like it was all in her head."

Samantha thought about how similar that story was to
her own experience as a social worker. Pain, guilt, shame,
resentment, and fear existed wholly in the brain. The
story you told yourself about yourself was the only one
you could really believe.

To other people, Kathy was a well-off teenager with a
million opportunities. But to Kathy, she was suffocated
and lost under the pressure of her parents, and drugs had
seemed like the only place to turn, a place to numb her
pain.

Over the next several days, Samantha kept up a similar
schedule. She worked tirelessly, meeting with her clients,
doing group sessions at the Nantucket Recovery House,
then completing her paperwork in her office before heading
off to the Jessabelle House to see the guys' progress.

Through it all, she reminded herself, over and over again, that life after Daniel would be worthwhile. She continued to sleep in the apartment, which didn't seem so bad now that it wasn't her forever home. In fact, it was sort of cute to live in such a small place, to listen to music only she liked on her speakers, and to dance in her underwear in the living room. Daniel hadn't liked being silly— not even when they'd been young. As a civil engineer, he'd needed everything to have a purpose, to have order, like her father had.

On the sixth day of construction, Samantha began to notice real progress. Derek showed her the new cabinets they'd installed, and she opened and closed them a few times, imagining herself years in the future doing it without thought. It was clear the brothers knew what they were doing— that their father had taught them well.

On the veranda, as a vibrant sun dunked into the ocean, Samantha allowed herself to look at the silly dating app Sharon had told her about. One after another, she swiped left, meaning "no." It felt like a game. Strange to think every single face she saw now had an entire story behind it. Every single man had lived life, had opinions and memories, and had dreams for their future. It felt crass to dismiss them.

Gosh, she felt old. When she'd met Daniel in college, everything had felt simple. Her life had fallen into place as organically as an apple grew from a tree. There was nothing natural about meeting a person on an app.

Then again, both Darcy and Rachelle had told her this was "the new normal."

"How's it going?" Derek's deep voice came from behind her.

Samantha nearly jumped from her skin. She quickly

shoved her phone into her pocket and turned to smile at him as he approached. It was the end of the workday, and he'd helped himself to one of the beers she kept in a cooler on the veranda.

"It's really something, isn't it?" Derek nodded at the sunset and sipped his beer. Although it was still only May, he already had a gorgeous tan.

"I can't believe this place is mine," Samantha admitted.

"Yeah. I had no idea it was possible to own the sunset," Derek teased.

"My aunt Jessabelle had that written into her will. 'And to my darling niece, Samantha— I give you the sun.'" Samantha made her voice deep and important.

"Dang. And here I thought we were lucky to have inherited my dad's construction company," Derek said.

"So you've done this full-time since you graduated high school?" Samantha asked.

"God, no." Derek laughed. "I own a fishing charter business. That's my real calling."

"Oh!" This explained the tan. "I had no idea. So, you just do this part-time?"

Derek grimaced and glanced back at the house. It was clear there was something more to the story. "My brothers love this work. They want to keep the family business alive a bit more than me, I guess. But then again, I like working with them. We went a few years without much contact, and it's been good to reconnect."

Samantha nodded, both surprised and grateful he'd told her. "Why did you lose contact? You don't have to answer that if it's too personal."

Derek rubbed his fingers through his lush hair. "It's a

long story. I'm sure it's one you've heard over and over again, being a social worker and all."

Before Samantha had a chance to answer, Patrick's voice came from inside the house. "Hey! Samantha! Are you there?"

Samantha jumped toward the open window and hollered into the house. "You okay, Patrick?"

"I think I found something!" Patrick called.

Samantha and Derek locked eyes. *Had Patrick heard them talking?* It was impossible; he was all the way downstairs. Still, it felt strange and exhilarating that Derek had suddenly differentiated himself from his brothers, as though he'd wanted to share a piece of his soul with her.

Samantha and Derek headed inside and down the staircase, where they found Patrick in front of a brick wall. Two of the bricks had been removed to make space for a small cabinet.

"Oh my gosh!" Samantha cried. "What is that?"

"I just moved this bookcase to the side and found this." When they'd arrived, the bookcase had been heavy with dusty tomes and old dictionaries, which Darcy and Rachelle had cleaned and put in boxes.

"Creepy," Brent said from behind them. "Was your aunt into treasure maps? Or the occult?"

"Not that I know of," Samantha said.

"You do the honors." Patrick stepped back and gestured for her to approach.

Samantha took a sharp breath and bent down to grab the small knob. It took very little strength to tug it open. When she did, she found the cabinet filled with old brown books.

"I'm sorry to say there's no money back here, gentlemen," she joked. Carefully, she removed the first book to the left and opened it to find Aunt Jessabelle's gorgeous cursive handwriting. Her heart doubled in size. "My gosh. I had no idea she kept diaries."

"That's a real treasure," Derek pointed out. "There's what? Fifteen of them?"

Samantha was captivated. It was as though her aunt Jessabelle hadn't been done telling her everything she'd wanted to say. There were so many stories left to share and so much of her personality to understand. There in the old living room, Samantha closed her eyes and thanked Aunt Jessabelle, wherever she was, for giving her such an incredible gift.

For what better gift is there than truly understanding someone you love?

Chapter Seven

1968

J essabelle had married late. Everyone said so behind her back and also to her face because the wants and needs of a woman were always second fiddle to the wants and needs of everyone else. Still, Jessabelle, who was now thirty-three years old, wasn't embarrassed to say how pleased she was to have Arnold as her husband. Arnold was kind, compassionate, handsome, and intelligent— and he seemed to really "get" her. The only problem, really, was that although they'd been trying since they'd gotten married, Jessabelle was still not pregnant.

It was the afternoon of the solstice party. For as long as she could remember, Jessabelle's family had always held solstice parties to celebrate the beginning of summer. They invited the most sophisticated, well-dressed, and affluent people of Nantucket Island to their home, where they hobnobbed and talked about how much money they made and eventually got drunk and watched fireworks.

In previous years, the solstice party had annoyed Jessabelle, as it meant more time for everyone to ask her when she planned to get married. *"Time is running out,"* so many had said. This year was different. She had Arnold for protection.

Jessabelle had agreed to meet Margaret at their parents' place outside Siasconset a few hours before the party began. Jessabelle's sister Margaret was two years older than she was but already had two boys, Grant, age fifteen, and Roland, age thirteen. They were entering the experimental phase of their teen lives, and Jessabelle knew Marg would have her hands full. Because Margaret's husband, Chuck, was fully devoted to his career and spent so much time away, Margaret had recently returned to work as a nurse at the Nantucket Hospital, which she called "incredibly exhilarating and rewarding work." Jessabelle was terribly proud of her sister. There was no one on earth she loved more.

Now, Arnold dropped Jessabelle off at the house where she'd grown up, kissed her, and said, "I'll see you at the party later." Jessabelle hopped out and waved to Margaret, who lay in the sun on the veranda, wearing a pair of sunglasses and a beautiful summer dress.

"Aren't you a sight for sore eyes," Jessabelle said as she hurried up the steps to the veranda.

Margaret giggled and stood to hug Jessabelle. "Sit down! It's been ages since we saw each other." Margaret gestured toward the seat beside her and turned to pour Jessabelle a glass of lemonade. "Tell me everything. How's the library? How's Arnold?"

Jessabelle sipped her lemonade and sat. Through the

window, she saw her mother, who styled her hair in the mirror.

"The library is a dream," Jessabelle said. "I'm surrounded by books and people who actually like to read them constantly."

"Gosh. I imagine it'll be so hard to leave when you have children," Margaret said.

"Yes. Absolutely." Jessabelle continued to smile. *Why hadn't she told Margaret about her fertility struggles? They'd always told each other everything. Was she ashamed?*

"Father and Mother brag about your wedding endlessly," Margaret said. "I have to admit it makes me jealous. I got married when I was nineteen and deliriously in love. I had no plans for my life at all. It's frankly a miracle that I finished nursing school in the first place."

"I'm so glad you did," Jessabelle said. "I'm sure Chuck is proud of you."

Margaret waved flippantly. "Chuck's never been proud of anyone but himself."

Jessabelle arched her eyebrow, struck with Margaret's strange mood. Margaret hardly spoke ill of her husband. *Was there something wrong at home?*

"Girls?" Their mother appeared in the doorway to the veranda and grinned at them nervously. "I wondered if you could help me with the hors d'oeuvres for this evening."

"It's why we're here, Mother!" Jessabelle replied.

Together, Jessabelle and Margaret followed their mother into the beautiful Victorian home, which had been designed by Charles H. Robinson, the architect who'd popularized the architectural style across Nantucket Island. As a child, Jessabelle hadn't fully appreciated the way the house was designed, but she fully adored it now. Out on that veranda, especially, the air was fresh with the smells of the sea, and the sun was soul-affirming.

In the kitchen, Margaret and Jessabelle fell into an easy rhythm with their mother. They gossiped and laughed, slicing bread for tiny sandwiches, sautéing onions, and making bite-sized chocolate and vanilla desserts. Their mother pestered Jessabelle frequently about Arnold, asking her questions about her "homemaking" abilities that irritated Jessabelle to no end.

"I've taken care of myself all these years, Mother," she finally said. "What makes you think I can't take care of a home just because Arnold also happens to live in it?"

Her mother's cheeks lost all their color. After a moment, she stuttered, then said, "Very well," and disappeared from the kitchen for a moment. Margaret patted Jessabelle's shoulder and said, "I love that you stand up for yourself." Still, Jessabelle was left wondering if she shouldn't have, as it had clearly upset their mother.

By five, guests began to arrive for the solstice party. Chuck Coleman, Margaret's husband, came early with a pack of beer and a smile that said he ruled the world. His arrogance was always second to none. Margaret kissed him dutifully on the cheek and asked him questions about Roland and Grant, who would be arriving soon with friends of the family.

Arnold came soon afterward. He kissed Jessabelle on the lips and complimented her dress. "You must be the prettiest lady here by a mile," he whispered into her ear.

Jessabelle blushed and swatted him playfully on the shoulder. "And you must be the biggest liar."

"Arnold, my man." Chuck stepped forward to shake

Arnold's hand. "I hope you're still considering my offer to join my company?"

Chuck was a well-respected stock trader. According to Margaret, he made "buckets" of money and was frequently needed for business trips in New York City and throughout the rest of New England. Arnold was an academic who wrote newspaper articles for very niche journals. They couldn't have been more different.

"I'm afraid I'm too enamored with my own career," Arnold confessed.

Chuck eyed Jessabelle curiously. "You've told him what glories await him at my company, haven't you?"

Jessabelle wanted to roll her eyes but didn't. "Arnold is a man of the written word."

"A man who rejects the gold he's been offered," Chuck corrected. "A fool!" He laughed and smacked Arnold on the shoulder. "Come. Have a cigar with me, at least."

Arnold followed after Chuck, leaving Margaret and Jessabelle alone. Before Jessabelle could speak, Roland and Grant appeared. They were long-legged and good-looking boys, clearly from a well-respected and rich family. Although Roland's knees had grass stains, the rest of him was clean-cut.

"What have you done to yourself?" Margaret said with a sigh. Under her breath, she said, "Mother is going to kill me. It's the solstice party, for goodness' sake!" She dropped down and began to scrub Roland's knees with her thumb.

"He's thirteen, Marg. Don't you want him to enjoy his summer?" Jessabelle locked eyes with Roland. "Why don't you go into the bathroom and try to clean yourself up? For your mother's sake."

Roland considered this and eyed his older brother, Grant. The boys were thick as thieves and seemed to speak in silent code.

"We'll be back," Grant affirmed as he led Roland away.

"We should refill the punch bowl." Margaret turned on her heel and headed for the kitchen. Jessabelle followed behind.

As they mixed another round of punch, the band their father had hired for the evening began to play. They'd set up at a distance from the house and party, and the sounds of their string instruments swelled over the dunes. Jessabelle's eyes filled with tears at the music, although she wasn't sure why. Perhaps it had something to do with the laughter from the children at the party, which echoed through the air. *When would her own children join them?*

Perhaps everyone in her family had been correct. Perhaps she shouldn't have focused so many years on her career. Perhaps she should have married the first or second guy who had shown interest in her, had a few children, and then considered her academic worth.

"Are you okay, Sis?" Margaret smiled, rubbing Jessabelle's arm.

"Yes, I'm just fine," Jessabelle lied, feigning a small grin.

"Chuck seems to like Arnold," Margaret tried.

"Yeah." Jessabelle wasn't sure if that was true.

Out the window, they watched as more and more guests arrived. They greeted one another with handshakes and cheek-kisses, complimenting outfits and asking about sailboats and real estate prices. For not the first time, the sheer amount of wealth twisted Jessabelle's stomach.

"Oh. I hadn't realized he was coming." Margaret's face changed, and Jessabelle followed her gaze out the window toward a handsome man in his late thirties. He smiled and handed a bottle of champagne to their father.

"Who is that?" Jessabelle asked.

Margaret spoke quickly. "That is Dr. Trevor Rushford. I work for him at the hospital."

Margaret had never spoken of a Dr. Rushford. Jessabelle arched her eyebrow and followed Margaret outside, where they restocked the punch and several snacks. Margaret played with her hair, attempting to smooth it. She then turned just in time to say, "Good evening, Dr. Rushford. So good to see you again."

Jessabelle listened intently. Her sister's voice wavered. Something was amiss.

"It's always a pleasure to be invited to the solstice party," Dr. Trevor Rushford said.

"Yes. We look forward to it." Margaret paused. "My husband is just around the corner, smoking a cigar with a few other men. You should join them."

"Perhaps I will. I never turn down a fine cigar."

Suddenly, strong arms wrapped around Jessabelle's waist. Arnold kissed her neck and whispered, "Gosh, I hate cigars."

Jessabelle laughed and turned into him. Suddenly, he had his hand around hers, and they began to dance, swaying with the music. Margaret disappeared somewhere, leaving them alone.

"I hope it wasn't too horrible to talk to Chuck," Jessabelle said softly.

Arnold shook his head. "Chuck isn't that bad. He's just got a huge ego since his career took off, but honestly, who wouldn't? He'll cool down sooner than later when he realizes there is more to life."

"You think?" Jessabelle asked.

Arnold shrugged. "No idea."

They laughed gently, gazing into one another's eyes. Jessabelle wasn't sure if she'd ever been happier than when she was in his arms. Perhaps they didn't have to have children to be happy. Perhaps they could just read and write into old age.

The night continued. Mostly, Jessabelle stuck close to Arnold, sipping wine and chatting with friends and acquaintances. Margaret weaved in and out of the crowds, sometimes with Chuck and sometimes without. At the far end of the party, Grant and Roland played football with several of the other kids, getting more grass stains by the minute. Nobody seemed to mind. They were teen boys. That's what they did.

After it got dark, Jessabelle and Arnold danced and whispered about wanting to go home, to get away from "all this ruckus." Jessabelle thought fireworks were slightly outrageous, and Arnold wanted to finish writing an article that was due in a few days.

As they spoke, something caught Jessabelle's eye behind Arnold's shoulder. Slowly, she lifted onto her tiptoes to catch the moonlight against Margaret's blond hair. Directly in front of Margaret was a strong figure, a man. If she wasn't mistaken, Margaret's hand was around his upper arm.

Was that Chuck?

But no. On cue, Chuck's laughter boomed from directly behind Jessabelle. Jessabelle's heart burned with curiosity. *Was that Dr. Rushford?*

"What's wrong?" Arnold asked.

Jessabelle waved off her husband. She couldn't share her suspicions. Although she loved Arnold, Margaret's life and Margaret's secrets were more important than anything.

"Nothing," Jessabelle said softly. "You know I love you. And I'm so happy you want to leave this terrible party just as much as I do."

"We're a match made in heaven," Arnold agreed.

Chapter Eight

Present Day

I t was late May on Nantucket Island, and Samantha had decided it was time to start sleeping part-time at the Jessabelle House. To prepare, she ordered a brand-new bed frame and mattress and had them delivered on a Friday afternoon. With the new bed set up and the last of the Friday light shimmering through the windowpane, she was struck with a new brand of hope.

This bed wasn't the bed she'd ever shared with Daniel. This bed was completely her own. And she could sleep directly in the center if she wanted to.

"Looks comfortable." Derek appeared in the bedroom doorway and smiled. Downstairs, one of the other brothers used a power tool, and the sound roared through the house.

"I can really only sleep if someone is using a power

tool in the house," Samantha joked. "Do you think one of you can stay overnight?"

Derek laughed. "Our overnight rates are pretty steep."

"I was afraid of that." Samantha hopped out of the bedroom and stepped onto the veranda. She could feel Derek following behind her; it was as though he hung on her every word. A part of her had already begun to fear the day they finished the Jessabelle House. Derek had become her source of laughter and joy.

"You said the oven and stovetop are up and running?" Samantha turned back to lock eyes with Derek.

"They're ready to go," Derek affirmed.

"I was hoping to keep the three of you for dinner tonight," Samantha said. "You've been working so hard the past couple of weeks, and it doesn't feel right to feed you only sandwiches and beer."

"You don't have to do that."

"I'd love to. I mean, only if you can manage it. I'm sure you all have Friday night plans," Samantha said. *Was she digging for more information about Derek's private life?* He hadn't mentioned a girlfriend, but that didn't mean anything.

"Let me talk to the guys," Derek said. "But I've never known them to turn down a free meal."

Not long afterward, Rachelle and Darcy drove up the long driveway. Miraculously, Rachelle had the night off from the restaurant, and they'd decided to swing by to help cook Samantha's smorgasbord.

"I'm sure you have no desire to cook anything else," Samantha said as she squeezed Rachelle.

"I live to cook!" Rachelle countered. "I just hope you have good knives. I can't work with bad equipment."

Samantha had begun to bring bits and pieces from her old life to her new one. For that night's dinner, she'd retrieved skillets, baking pans, spatulas, very sharp knives, and plenty of plates and glasses from the storage facility. It was remarkable to see them in the fresh cabinets, as though they'd been made for them.

As Darcy sliced onions, she asked, "How long has this house been in the family again?"

"Honestly, it's hard to say," Samantha said. "Great-Aunt Jessabelle was given this house by her father. She and her sister grew up here."

"And her sister was your grandma Margaret?" Rachelle asked.

Samantha nodded. She'd begun to prepare the chicken and had rolled up her sleeves to her elbows. It occurred to her that she, Rachelle, and Darcy prepared dinner in the same kitchen where Margaret and Jessabelle had prepared the hors d'oeuvres for the solstice party back in 1968, which Samantha had just read about in one of the diaries.

"But Grandma Margaret died very young," Samantha explained. "She was only fifty-one."

Rachelle and Darcy had heard this before, surely, but they still looked stricken.

"That's really young. How did she die?" Rachelle asked.

"It was a heart attack," Samantha said. "Although Aunt Jessabelle always said she died of a broken heart."

Darcy furrowed her brow. "Why was her heart broken?"

"I'm not sure, honey," Samantha returned with a weak smile. "She never elaborated. Although, based on the diary entries, I'm starting to think my grandma

65

Margaret and grandpa Chuck's marriage wasn't exactly a healthy one."

Rachelle and Darcy looked at each other with wide eyes.

"We told you to tell us everything you learned in the diaries!" Rachelle cried.

Suddenly, Derek and Patrick popped out from the next room.

"We told you that too!" Patrick added with a laugh. "Come on. You're doing a deep dive into your family's history, which is almost one hundred years old. It's fascinating stuff. You have to share."

"Give us just one weird detail from the diaries," Derek demanded as he leaned against the doorframe.

"All right! All right." Samantha held her hands up in mock surrender, then grinned. It felt as though they kept Aunt Jessabelle alive with these stories. "All my life, everyone told me my great-aunt Jessabelle had never married. Aunt Jessabelle herself told me that she had never wanted to marry anyone, as it meant giving up her freedom. Well, it turns out she actually was married to a guy named Arnold. Isn't that wild?"

"You're kidding," Rachelle said.

"She told us that too!" Darcy cried. "I can't believe she lied about that."

"The marriage must have ended quickly, or something happened," Derek pointed out. "Otherwise, she wouldn't have covered it up all these years."

"I can understand why someone would want to hide from their past," Patrick added. "I mean, it's hard to admit when you've lost something. The loss becomes so much more real when you say it out loud."

Everyone nodded contemplatively.

"I've also learned a bit more about my grandpa Chuck," Samantha admitted. "It's strange. After Grandma Margaret died, I have no memories of him at all. All I know is he and my father didn't see eye to eye at all."

"How does he seem in the diaries?" Rachelle asked.

"Jessabelle doesn't seem like the biggest fan of him," Samantha explained. "She describes him as loud, arrogant, and always smoking cigars."

"Ew," Darcy said.

Suddenly, Brent appeared in the doorway, his smile crooked. "Wait, did I just miss a big reveal from the diaries?"

Everyone laughed. Samantha waved them out with a towel and said, "I'll tell you more at dinner. Go! Wash your hands! Grab a beer! Let's enjoy ourselves for once in our lives."

On the veranda, Samantha set up two card tables and chairs, all of which she'd taken from storage. Darcy and Rachelle set the tables as the three brothers sat to chat and watch the sunset ooze into pinks and oranges along the horizon. When it was time, Samantha hurried to the veranda with a big platter of butter chicken and fresh naan.

"I hope you don't mind a bit of experimentation," she said to the brothers.

"It smells so good!" Patrick cried. His eyes were slightly glassy. He stood quickly and grabbed himself another beer, then sat at one of the card tables. Samantha noticed that Derek followed him with his eyes.

"It really does," Derek agreed after a moment. He poured himself some water and sat across from Patrick as

Brent took the end. This left the other three seats for Samantha, Darcy, and Rachelle.

Together, the six of them toasted the sunset, the Jessabelle House, and the approaching summer. Their forks clinked against the plates, and silence fell as they engaged with the spices and thick sauces, and perfectly cooked chicken.

"You've outdone yourself, Mom," Rachelle said between bites.

This was a wonderful compliment coming from Rachelle. On top of that, both of Samantha's daughters knew that their father hadn't been keen on experimentation in the kitchen. Rachelle had gotten away with it, being Daniel's daughter. But when Samantha attempted new things, Daniel ridiculed her and said, *"Why don't you just make what I like instead of this crap?"*

Very soon, Patrick got up and snagged another beer. This time, Samantha, Derek, and Brent followed him with their eyes. Nobody said anything about it. Patrick cracked his beer and smiled at Samantha with overwhelming goodwill.

"Okay. I'm going to need more info about the diaries," Patrick said.

Samantha was accustomed to addicts. It occurred to her for the first time that Patrick could have an issue, but it wasn't her business to pry, not now.

"All right. What else?" Samantha considered this. "Well, the year is 1968, and my aunt Jessabelle is pretty sure her sister, my grandmother, is cheating on her husband with a doctor at the hospital."

"Scandalous," Rachelle quipped as she lifted a glass of lemonade.

"Definitely," Samantha agreed. "Jessabelle realizes

that she and her sister actually have secrets from each other for the first time. It's bizarre for her, as she always thought they could tell each other everything."

"What is Jessabelle keeping from Margaret?" Derek asked.

"Apparently, she and her husband are having trouble getting pregnant," Samantha answered. After a pause, she added, "I had no idea how much she wanted children, but there's so much pain in her diary."

"How old was she in this diary?" Brent asked.

"Thirty-three," Samantha replied. "Which means I have a lot of her life left to read about."

When Patrick went to grab yet another beer, everyone watched but said nothing. When he sat, he cracked his beer and said, "I wish Dad would have left us a diary. It would have been great to know what he really thought about."

Everyone nodded. Brent talked about how he'd tried to start a diary but hadn't gotten into the swing of it. Rachelle said she tried to write down a few things every day, but sometimes that meant just writing a grocery list.

A little while later, Samantha heard herself say, "It's strange to learn about my family's past, especially because I've felt so ostracized from them my entire life. My father and I hardly talk, and my siblings have always thought I was the outcast in the family."

Sam saw the three brothers consider this with emotion in their eyes.

"You're the keeper of their secrets, now," Patrick slurred. He then stood and waddled toward the cooler on a mission.

But before Patrick could return to the table, Derek hurried to his feet and placed his hand on Patrick's shoulder. Under his breath, he said he needed to talk to Patrick. Samantha and her daughters kept their eyes down. This wasn't their business.

Inside came the sound of Patrick yelling at his brother to leave him alone. Brent smeared his mouth with his napkin and apologized. He then followed after them, ready to help.

Outside, Samantha and her daughters spoke in low voices.

"I hope he's okay," Rachelle said.

"He's such a lovely guy," Darcy said.

"He is," Samantha agreed. Her heart went out to the brothers, who had clearly been through this all before. She recognized the dynamic. Sam understood, now, part of the reason why Derek had said they'd lost touch.

Again, she remembered that Derek hadn't wanted to get back into the construction world. He'd done this for his brothers. *Had he wanted to keep a better eye on Patrick? Or did Patrick just have trouble holding down a job otherwise?*

A moment later, Brent and Derek appeared on the veranda. They smiled nervously.

"I think we'd better get back home," Derek said.

"We can't thank you enough for dinner." Brent palmed his neck.

"Of course. Any time." Samantha stood and hugged them both. She tried not to notice the intensity she felt as she brought Derek's body closer to hers. "Get home safe."

From the veranda, Samantha and her daughters watched as the construction truck eased down the long driveway and disappeared. Samantha's heartbeat felt very slow.

"It's remarkable that they're there for each other like

this," she said, thinking again of her own siblings. "I can't imagine what it must be like to have that support."

Rachelle and Darcy grabbed their mother's hands over the table. After a long pause, Darcy said, "You know we have your back, Mom. Right?"

"In everything," Rachelle affirmed.

Samantha nodded, her heart still bruised. How could she tell her daughters that they weren't meant to care for her? That forever, in Samantha's mind, she would do anything for them but never expect the same from them.

Because, unlike her father, she didn't put unwarranted expectations on her children. She'd promised herself she never would.

Chapter Nine

That weekend was one for the books. Samantha, Darcy, and Rachelle continued to flesh out the Jessabelle House to personalize it and make it uniquely their own. Samantha reminded her daughters continually that although they lived in a separate apartment, she wanted them to think of the Jessabelle House as theirs— a place to lay roots, for peace, good conversation, and love. For this reason, she'd ordered two additional bed frames with mattresses and told her daughters to pick their bedrooms. The plan was to decorate each with her daughters in mind— to uphold the beauty and sophistication of Darcy and the artistry of Rachelle with perfectly chosen paint colors and furnishings. Her daughters couldn't wait to get started.

Although there was only so much Samantha could do to refurbish the old place, she still found there were endless choices to make. *Did she want to keep most of Aunt Jessabelle's antique furnishings? How much of Jessabelle did she want to "feel" in each room?*

Already, she'd told the landlord of her apartment that

she planned to break the lease by the end of July. This allowed her to transition from the apartment to the Jessabelle House at her own pace. She thought of herself like a tide rising slowly into the Jessabelle House. Someday, it would feel as though she had always belonged.

Sunday evening, Rachelle and Darcy left Samantha at the Jessabelle House to meet friends in downtown Nantucket. This left Samantha on the veranda alone with a bottle of wine and a million swirling thoughts. As usual, she committed time to Jessabelle's diary and read more about what it had been like for her at thirty-three and thirty-four, years when she'd been hopelessly in love with a man named Arnold. It was funny to compare Jessabelle's love for Arnold to Samantha's own love for Daniel. When they'd first been married, Samantha had felt like Daniel was the only person on earth. She'd lost track of friends; she'd wanted to be with him every moment.

As she read, her phone buzzed with a text. Samantha finished a diary entry and then turned her attention to her phone. It was from Derek! Excitement throttled through her. It was rare he texted her about anything but construction scheduling.

> DEREK: Hey. I just wanted to apologize for the other night. I'm assuming, based on your career, that you understood what was happening.

> DEREK: I hope you know that we have it under control. Nothing will affect the work we do at the Jessabelle House.

Samantha's heartbeat intensified.

> SAMANTHA: Hi, Derek. I was worried about you, but I understand that these kinds of things are very sensitive. I didn't want to say anything.

> SAMANTHA: I have loved having you and your brothers around the Jessabelle House. The work and company have been superb. I definitely don't want to end our working relationship.

> SAMANTHA: But I hope you know that I am here for you if you need me. As you said, this is something I know quite a bit about. Families and addiction can be tough to get through.

Derek wrote back instantly.

> DEREK: Thank you for saying all that, Sam. I really appreciate your empathy.

> DEREK: Again, I hope everything will turn out fine.

> DEREK: Anyway. Hope to see you tomorrow. We should arrive around ten, like always.

After they finished their text exchange, Samantha refilled her glass of wine and watched the light play across the water for a while. Although she adored the old house, she'd very rarely been there by herself, and the feeling felt strange. She trusted it would subside over time. *How had Jessabelle been able to stand being alone all the time?*

Then again, Samantha was pretty sure being alone was something you had to practice. You had to get used to hearing only the voices in your head.

As if on cue, Sharon texted Samantha with a photograph of a guy from one of the apps.

> SHARON: I'm going out with this guy tonight! Wish me luck.

Samantha wrinkled her nose, wished Sharon good luck, and put her phone on airplane mode. Again, she turned to Jessabelle's diary, wondering if Jessabelle's failed marriage and subsequent decision to be single forever would teach Samantha how to live. Perhaps Jessabelle's strength would invigorate her own.

* * *

The next morning, Samantha woke at the Jessabelle House around six thirty. For the first time at the new place, she dressed in running shorts and a tank top and went for a run. Her thighs screamed, and her hair fell from its ponytail and flowed out behind her. When age had caught up to them, Daniel had told Samantha she had to start exercising. "You have to keep your metabolism up," he'd said, as though he was a doctor rather than a civil engineer. This led Samantha to detest exercise. It had felt like her husband's prescription rather than her idea.

Now, she ran most mornings for the fresh air and the invigorating feeling it left her when she was done, gasping for air. Of course, the exercise was a bonus as well. She stood on the beach and gasped for breath as the wind rushed across her cheeks. Miraculously, it was almost June, and summer bubbled to the surface.

She'd been alive forty-five years. She'd been given so many chances and seen so many things. But she wasn't done yet, dang it. Even Daniel, in his high-rise apartment building with his thirty-four-year-old girlfriend, couldn't tell her to stop.

But a surprise awaited her at the Jessabelle House.

As she mounted the hill, a familiar car sat in the driveway. Beside it stood a well-dressed man with slicked-back hair. He looked impatient and jittery, and he studied the Jessabelle House as though daring himself to go up to it.

When Samantha called out, "Dad?" he jumped with fear.

"Oh. Samantha." Roland shook his head and stepped back. "You went for a run."

Samantha had no idea why he was there. Sweat pooled under her armpits and on her back.

"I didn't expect company." Samantha's tone was formal.

"And I didn't expect that you'd moved in already," Roland quipped.

Samantha cocked her head. "So, you just wanted to come here and look at the house?"

Roland was quiet for a moment. It was difficult to know if he was ever embarrassed. "It's looking quite good. It spent a few years in disarray."

"I hired a small construction company," Samantha explained.

"Hodgers Construction?"

"No. Elrod and Sons."

"Oh." Roland seemed not to approve, but that was typical. "Yes, well. I suppose I should have hired someone years ago to come to refurbish it rather than let it get to the state it was in."

This surprised Samantha. She'd never known him to come out to Aunt Jessabelle's house or care about it at all.

Roland palmed the back of his neck. Stuttering, he

explained, "I never could come back out here after Mom died. Too many memories in the old place. She was raised here, you know. And we used to have the solstice parties here before your mother and I took over."

Samantha furrowed her brow. It was very rare for her father to open up like this. *What had gotten into him?* There was a softness in his eyes as though he was flooded with memories.

"I've been thinking about Aunt Jessabelle and Grandma Margaret's relationship lately," Samantha confessed. For some reason, she didn't want to tell her father about the diaries.

Roland locked eyes with her.

"I mean, they were thicker than thieves, right?" Samantha asked, returning his gaze. "Aunt Jessabelle said Margaret was her dearest friend and closest companion in her life. She said she was heartbroken when she died."

Roland nodded, misty-eyed. "My mother was a wonderful woman. I wish you could have gotten to know her better."

Samantha raised one of her shoulders. "I was young she died, but I do have some memories. More than anything, I wish I could have been able to sit with her and ask her so many questions. When you're a kid, you don't have any concept of death, or you shouldn't, at least. But in that way, I never considered she wouldn't be around much longer."

Roland now looked at Samantha as though he'd never seen her before. She felt very strange and open-hearted. Was this really the man who despised her and had told her he would never respect her or her career or any of her decisions?

But in the same breath, he was now a sixty-seven-year-old man. He'd lived, and he'd lost. Mysteries hovered in his past— ones Samantha felt on the verge of cracking.

And for the first time, it occurred to her that somewhere in the diaries, she would probably find out why her father had stopped all contact with her grandpa Chuck. This had been one of the biggest mysteries in her life.

How damaged was her father? How much trauma did he carry around with him?

Suddenly, Samantha heard herself speak. "Dad?"

"Yes?" Roland looked so tender and broken.

"I'm just curious about something. You don't have to answer. But, did you ever hear something about Grandma Margaret having an affair with a doctor at the hospital she worked at?"

Suddenly, Roland's eyes turned to slits. He looked at Samantha as though she was the devil incarnate. "Where on earth did you get that idea from?"

Samantha stuttered. "Oh... Umm...I don't know. I don't have any specific proof. I just—"

But Roland interrupted her. "I don't know why you would speak ill of your grandmother like this. I know you were quite young when we lost her, but I always thought you loved your grandma Margaret."

"I did love her. I do love her." Samantha felt panicked.

"She never should have died," Roland muttered angrily. "It was all his fault. It's always been his fault." He gazed out across the horizon, lost in thought.

Samantha was at a loss. Whatever goodwill they'd built up in the past few minutes was now lost again. On top of that, she had to shower and leave for work.

"I have to get ready," Samantha said tentatively. She stepped around him, keeping a healthy distance. When she reached the steps to head up to the veranda, she turned to look at him again. She half expected him to ridicule her job or say something about how she'd wasted her life in her profession. Instead, he continued to stare out at the water.

Why had Margaret's affair affected him so much? If he loved his mother so much and hated his father so much, couldn't he understand why his mother might have wanted to cheat on his father?

Then again, he was Roland Coleman. Roland Coleman needed everything to be absolutely perfect, even fifty years after the fact. He couldn't stand anything or anyone to taint his family's name.

"Well. Bye, Dad. Always a pleasure." Samantha turned and rushed up the steps, overwhelmed with emotion. By the time she stood beneath the stream of water in the only shower the brothers had up and running, she shivered with rage. Roland had been the first man to ever tell her just how wrong she was. In his eyes, she'd chosen her path when she'd chosen not to follow the family business. Now, he'd decided to roll up to her new house whenever he pleased. *How the heck was she supposed to heal if he could come down the driveway at any moment?*

Chapter Ten

1970

It had been over two years since Jessabelle had seen her sister, Margaret, sneak off with Doctor Trevor Rushford at the solstice party of 1968. Still, Margaret hadn't mentioned the affair. Not once.

By now, Jessabelle and Arnold had been married for over two years. Despite endlessly trying, she was thirty-five and still childless. The look in Arnold's eyes had begun to alarm her. Although they still spoke of art, music, and movies, and although they still dined out together and went on long walks, there was a dullness to his gaze. *Had he decided to give up on her giving him a child? Was extending his line something he desperately needed?*

Would he go somewhere else to fix that issue?

Jessabelle had thrown herself into work at the library, quietly rising in the ranks. People no longer regarded her as a beautiful woman, but rather, they regarded her as strong and intellectually powerful. Although she liked this feeling, it felt strange to say goodbye to a time in her life when people had opened doors for her, complimented the dresses she wore, and asked her when she would fall in love. It felt as though time had passed her by.

It was late August, and Jessabelle agreed to meet Margaret at a beach near the home they'd grown up in. Margaret had said she would pack a picnic. Jessabelle stopped at the nearby grocery store to buy a bottle of wine. As she drove to the beach, memories from Jessabelle's childhood washed over, forcing her to pull over to the side of the road to cry. "What is wrong with me?" she muttered as she cleaned up her makeup.

It was time for Jessabelle to confess to her sister just how lonely she felt. It was time to explain how desperately she wanted children. She couldn't carry this burden alone any longer.

Down the beach, Margaret sat in a yellow bikini. Her picnic basket was closed beside her in the sand, and her blond curls tossed in the wind. Jessabelle hurried to her and fell on the towel, grateful for this time away from men and families.

"Look at you!" Margaret smiled and took Jessabelle's hands. "I hope you packed your swimsuit?"

Jessabelle changed into a red bikini. Together, the sisters danced beneath the sun as though they were seventeen instead of thirty-five and thirty-seven. They then joined hands and charged into the water, yelping as it splashed over them. Out there in the water and beneath the sun, Jessabelle's issue with conceiving was no longer at the front of her mind. In fact, she hardly had to think at all.

Margaret unpacked the salad, fruit, and sandwiches as Jessabelle poured wine. For a little while, they spoke about simple things such as the price of cheese and Roland's newly discovered anger, and their parents' nagging. Always, their parents seemed to have something to nag about, no matter the girls' ages.

But just as Jessabelle opened her lips to finally tell someone about her childless life, Margaret burst into tears. Her face was tomato-red, and she scrunched it up like a child.

Jessabelle's heart burst with pity. Her first thoughts were horrible. *Did Margaret have cancer? Was there something wrong with the children?*

"I'm sorry," Margaret sputtered as Jessabelle tried to console her. "I'm just so sorry."

"What is it?" Jessabelle wrapped her arm around Margaret and held her close. "You can tell me anything. You know that."

Margaret rubbed her eyes, smearing her makeup. "I just don't know what to do. I really don't." After another sigh, she came out with it. "I've done something horrible, Jessabelle. Really horrible."

Jessabelle's eyes widened. *Was this it? Was she finally going to tell her?*

"Chuck is a wonderful husband. He is. But since he opened the second office on Martha's Vineyard, he's just been so consumed with it, rather than the boys and I. It's been like this for a long, long time. I told myself that our new dynamic wouldn't be forever, but when the boys got a little older, as you know, I went back to the hospital. And gosh, Jess. I fell in love with that job. Finally, it was like my work was actually necessary, rather than just another shirt to iron or toilet to clean. I kept people alive. I made people comfortable during their most difficult days. And I began to think of my life back at home as less-than and not fulfilling enough."

Jessabelle nodded. As a career woman, this made so much sense to her.

"Anyway, Dr. Rushford... I mean, Trevor's attention didn't alarm me at first. I thought it was fascinating that such a smart and handsome man was actually interested in talking to me. By then, I felt like yesterday's news, you know? But more and more, I dreamt of him. I couldn't wait to go to the hospital every day to see him. Gosh, when he smiled at me, I floated through the rest of the day.

"When we began the affair, Chuck was away on business yet again. I assumed I would be eaten up with guilt when he got back, but because he hardly looked at me, I was able to play housewife and pretend everything was fine. Slowly but surely, I felt myself build a double life.

"And then, just last week, Chuck took me aside. Roland and Grant were outside playing catch. I thought Chuck was going to tell me to iron his shirts a different way or clean the kitchen better or any number of other things I'm expected to do and do perfectly to uphold the Coleman reputation. Instead, he told me very coldly that I was embarrassing him. That I was shaming not just him but the entire Coleman family, and that I had to end the affair immediately."

Jessabelle's jaw dropped. "How did he find out?"

Margaret shook her head. "I have no idea. I thought I was being so careful."

Jessabelle considered telling Margaret that she'd known for over two years— that she and her handsome doctor clearly hadn't been very careful. But she kept this to herself.

"I told Trevor this morning that we have to end it," Margaret breathed. "But my heart is broken. I don't know if I'll be able to manage it. I see Trevor all the time. Meanwhile, Chuck has been and still takes off to all corners of New England, specifically Martha's Vineyard. It's enough to drive a woman wild."

Margaret's eyes were enormous, almost pleading. "Doesn't he understand how lonely I am? Doesn't he understand that I need a real, romantic relationship? Doesn't he understand that I married him for reasons that had nothing to do with homemaking and bread baking?" She smacked her naked thigh as tears streamed down her cheeks.

Jessabelle's heart ached for her sister. She held her, asking questions about Trevor, about the love Margaret had for both men.

"Oh, they're both so arrogant in their own right," Margaret said. "Handsome and so sure of themselves. They've been given the world. But Chuck is the father of my children. We've been through everything together. If only he'd commit his life to me the way I'm committed to him! I would never look at Trevor again."

Jessabelle furrowed her brow. "You said you left Trevor this morning?"

Margaret let out a sob. "We kissed afterward. He told me he wouldn't let me go that easily. And after that, I immediately called you. I needed to see you. I needed to know someone in this world still loved me after I confessed what I'd done. But I know I can't see Trevor again. I can't. And I guess that means I'll have to leave my job and go back to my normal house duties."

Minutes passed, then an hour. The light over the beach changed, becoming golden. Finally, just as she'd planned, Jessabelle found a way to tell her sister what was on her mind. She told her about her inability to get pregnant, how every month she hoped for a baby that never came. And although Margaret said she was so sorry, and that she loved her so much, and that she ached for her, Margaret also told her something Jessabelle would never forget.

"Don't have Arnold's children. He wants to trap you to take care of them, and then, he will never look at you the same way," she said resolutely.

Jessabelle knew that her sister was just reflecting her own life experiences onto her. Still, it was painful to hear.

Later that night, after she made sure Margaret was safe at home and in bed, Jessabelle drove back to the house she and Arnold had purchased when they'd married. The goal had been to fill it with children. Now, the guest bedrooms were filled with books and exercise equipment, and spare junk.

It was late. When Jessabelle entered the front door, there wasn't a sound. Slowly, she floated through the house like a ghost, checking the mail and drinking a glass of water. It was only when she reached the bedroom door upstairs that she realized Arnold was home. It was only when she opened the door that she realized he wasn't alone.

The panic on Arnold's and his lover's faces was another thing Jessabelle wouldn't forget. The woman was young, and she shrieked Arnold's name, fear marring her beautiful features. Arnold looked at Jessabelle and said, "I thought you said you were staying with Margaret," as though this was all her fault.

Jessabelle didn't have the strength to argue. She turned and walked down the hallway to one of the guest bedrooms. Behind the locked door, she listened as the young woman left and Arnold crept down the hallway. He knocked on the door, but she didn't answer. *What was there to say?* Due to her silence, Arnold began to whimper with sorrow.

"I'm sorry, Jessabelle. I'm sorry. I love you. I just can't do this. I can't do this anymore. It's too painful. Every month, it's like the universe is telling us we never should have gotten together. Maybe we just should have been friends, Jessabelle. You know? Maybe if we got divorced, we could just be the best of friends."

Chapter Eleven

Present Day

I t was June on Nantucket Island. The sun was a permanent fixture in the sky as sailboats buzzed across the Nantucket Sound and headed toward the Atlantic. Beautiful women in summer dresses ate ice cream cones on the boardwalk while lovers walked hand-in-hand on the beach, confident their love was more powerful than anyone else's. The horrendous winter was hardly a memory. The Nantucketers had made it through another season.

By the first week of June, Samantha had moved the majority of her personal things into the Jessabelle House. The apartment was now just a larger storage unit, a place where her belongings awaited her final decision: to throw away, to donate, or to keep.

Each week at the Jessabelle House brought the beautiful Victorian closer to the twenty-first century. The brothers worked diligently drilling, sanding, nailing, and painting. The "before" photos Samantha had taken prior to the beginning of the redesign proved just how tremendous the change was. Brent had even started work on the outside of the house, removing the old shutters and hanging new ones. As you drove up the driveway, the Jessabelle House seemed so much brighter with its new facelift; it glowed with what seemed like a heavenly blessing.

It was a Tuesday late-afternoon, and Samantha had returned to Nantucket from another trip to a rehab facility outside Boston. The meeting had been emotional. The client she'd visited had hurled insults at himself, his family, and even Samantha and the island at-large. With her clients, Samantha was hard as steel— but when she retreated to her car, she had allowed a few tears to fall.

As of late, Nantucket's drug intake had begun to boom. *Why had addictions escalated?* Samantha couldn't figure it out.

Of course, she knew there were many reasons people sought out drugs or alcohol in the first place. Often, they wanted to alleviate the pain of their own existence or numb themselves from the pain they experienced. Perhaps drug dealers had picked up on the general malaise of people today and brought more drugs to the island to meet the demand.

Despite Samantha's thoughts on the drug scene in Nantucket, there was little she could do. Samantha wasn't a police officer. She couldn't stake out a drug house. She couldn't interrogate a suspect. All she could do was take care of the result of all these horrors— the addicts who were left behind.

For reasons Samantha wasn't entirely sure of, she'd

agreed to meet a guy from a dating app. In the office, she changed into a light blue dress and styled her hair in the mirror as Sharon gasped with excitement.

"Your first date since your divorce! That's a big deal," Sharon said.

"It's just two people getting a drink," Samantha corrected. "I don't even know this guy."

"That's the point. Aren't you sick of everyone you know?" Sharon asked.

Samantha again allowed herself to think of the last time she'd seen Derek. It had been that morning as he'd stretched his arms along the cabinets in the downstairs bedroom, his large hands feeling the smooth wood. "You chose well, Sam. I would have picked the same for this bathroom," he'd said.

Samantha planned to meet Harry Hollins at the little wine bar near the boardwalk. According to his profile, Harry was a fifty-two-year-old accountant, a prolific sailor, and a fantastic cook. The photos weren't terrible. Mostly, they'd been taken on sailboats, wherein Harry's hair was tousled every which way, and his smile was electric.

Harry Hollins already sat at a little table on the corner terrace outside the wine bar. Samantha waved and hurried toward him, her heart in her throat. When she reached his table, he stood, and they hugged awkwardly. It was bizarre to touch someone you'd only ever encountered on the internet. Samantha wasn't a fan.

"Have you been here before?" Harry asked, gesturing vaguely toward the wine bar.

"A few times." Samantha grinned and then realized she had absolutely no idea what to talk about. *What did people say on dates? What had she said to Daniel when they'd had their first?* She'd been eighteen, for crying out loud. She'd probably talked about midterms.

Graciously, the server soon arrived to get their wine orders. Harry asked a number of questions about the wine list, most of which made Samantha think he was needlessly pretentious.

"I'll just have a chardonnay," Samantha said.

"Are you sure?" Harry stitched his eyebrows together. "The orange is exquisite. I've gone to this region in France."

Samantha looked at the server for help. After an awkward pause, she said, "Okay. Sure. I'll have the orange."

As the server headed back inside, Samantha cursed herself. Allowing men to tell her what to do was the old way. *Why had she allowed herself to slip back into that role so easily?*

Then again, it was difficult to break old habits. She told this to her clients all the time. *"You have to be patient with yourself."*

"So, tell me about yourself," Harry began. He folded his hands under his chin and looked at her intently.

Samantha felt as though he expected her to perform. "Um? I'm from Nantucket?"

Harry nodded. "Great. Must have been amazing to grow up here."

Not exactly, Samantha thought. The wine arrived, and Samantha drank it immediately. The tang of the orange wine was strange and unpalatable, at least to her, a more "inexperienced" wine drinker. *When could she make an excuse and leave?*

Harry told her where he'd been born and how he'd gotten into accounting. None of it was interesting or incredible. *Then again, how could it be?* Everyone was born, built a career, and had a story.

"Any kids?" Samantha asked.

"No. I wanted to be able to travel and sail as much as I could, which never really meant settling down and doing the kid thing. I do think I'd make a great father, though."

Arrogant, much? "Why do you think that?" Samantha asked.

"I'm organized. I have good discipline," Harry explained.

Samantha bubbled with laughter. Harry looked at her with surprise.

"I'm sorry?" Harry asked, clearly confused about why she'd laughed. He hadn't told her a joke.

But how could Samantha describe to him just how wrong he was about fatherhood? Yes, organization and discipline were important elements of parenting. But love, kindness, and compassion were kings. You had to be open to making mistakes, to make them often. And you had to be okay with putting your children above everything else. Your life, your needs, and your desires suddenly played second or third fiddle.

"Oh, sorry. I was just thinking about something else," Samantha explained away her laughter.

Harry furrowed his brow. He obviously didn't like that her mind was supposedly elsewhere.

For a little while, they spoke of easy things. Harry told her about the winds over the Nantucket Sound. He described in detail why he liked sailing so much. He also explained every step of his favorite meal to cook, which took a good chunk out of Samantha's life. Okay, so in actuality, Harry was the one who spoke of easy things as Samantha nodded along and tried not to glance at the clock that hung outside the wine bar. *Was this what it meant to date again?*

"It's cool that you like to cook," Samantha tried to get a word in. "My daughter just finished another semester at the Boston Culinary School."

Harry's eyes glittered. "I actually got into that school, but I decided to turn down the acceptance to go sailing around the world."

Samantha was amazed at how easy it was for him to turn the conversation back on himself. But as she stewed in anger toward him, she was reminded of so many other men in her life. She thought of Daniel, who'd talked endlessly of himself, his career, and his needs, all while belittling who she was as a person. She thought of Grandpa Chuck, who'd made Grandma Margaret feel so unloved that she'd had to seek validation and love outside her marriage. And then, she thought of this stranger named Arnold, who'd cheated on Great-Aunt Jessabelle and broken her heart.

Why had Samantha and so many intelligent women before her allowed these men to get away with this for so long?

Abruptly, Samantha stood. The table shook slightly in front of her. Harry looked at her as though he'd never seen her before. *Did he just word-vomit whatever he wanted to say on all his dates?*

"I have to use the bathroom," Samantha said. "Please excuse me."

Inside the ladies' room, Samantha studied her reflection. Her time spent on the Jessabelle House veranda had given her a healthy glow, and her hair had brightened with the summer sun, just as it always had since her childhood. With Harry outside waiting for her, she felt like a trapped animal. *How could she get out of this date?*

"Pull it together, Sam," she muttered to herself. "He's just some self-absorbed guy. He's not the boogeyman."

Correction— he wasn't Daniel or her father, and he didn't deserve any of her fear.

When Samantha reached the outdoor table, Harry was in conversation with the server about a region of Italy he'd recently traveled to. The server said all the right things.

"I'm so sorry," Samantha rasped. "I've just realized..."

Harry and the server looked at her. The server's eyes were wide, empathetic, as though she got it.

"I've just realized I can't be here." Samantha shrugged. She had no excuse, nor did she need one. "It was so nice to meet you." She placed a ten-dollar bill on the table and nodded at Harry, who looked flabbergasted. *Had nobody walked out on a date with him before?* "Take care."

With a rush of adrenaline, Samantha breezed out of the restaurant. The salty wind cooled her face as her thoughts calmed. By the time she reached the boardwalk and peered out across the harbor, she'd begun to smile to herself. She'd done it! She'd gone on a date! Oh, and she'd hated it.

Samantha texted Sharon a brief synopsis. Sharon wrote back that that sometimes happens and to just keep her chin up. But Samantha's chin was all the way up. Meeting Harry had allowed her to practice being the sort of woman she'd always wanted to be. Assertive, sure of herself, and more "Jessabelle-like."

As Samantha walked along the boardwalk, a surprise

call came through. A shiver ran up her spine when she read the name of the caller. It was Derek.

"Derek Elrod, as I live and breathe." She smiled into the phone, excited for their witty rapport.

But Derek's voice was flat and hard. "Hey, Samantha. I'm sorry to call you like this. I don't know who else to reach out to."

Samantha stopped along the boardwalk and gripped the railing. Something was very wrong.

"Patrick left work around lunchtime. He said he had an appointment, so we drove separately," Derek explained. "But he never came back. Brent and I have done everything. We've called his phone, checked his apartment, and even called a few friends, but we can't find him."

Samantha closed her eyes. This was certainly alarming. When Patrick had drunk too much beer on the night of the veranda dinner, Samantha had seen the hurt that had swirled in his eyes. He'd looked like a wounded animal.

There was something broken in him. He knew it. Everyone knew it.

"It's not just alcohol," Derek admitted then. "Back in Boston, it was other stuff too. Hard stuff. I didn't think he could get his hands on it here in Nantucket, but..."

Samantha's heart sank. If there was anything she knew, it was that you could get your hands on whatever you wanted. Nantucket had a smorgasbord of illegal substances. And Patrick had walked right into the trap.

Chapter Twelve

Samantha met Derek and Brent at Patrick's apartment. The place wasn't so far from her old place and had a similar energy— one bedroom, a kitchenette, and not a lot of hope. Brent was on Patrick's leather sofa with his face in his hands, and Derek paced the carpet. He looked stricken.

"I just thought things would be easier here," Derek muttered. "I thought we could keep an eye on him. I thought..."

"You can't blame yourself," Samantha urged him. "Addiction is a terrible thing. It's a horrible disease that your brother has to fight. I know you know your brother is not a bad person. In fact, he's just about the sweetest guy I've ever known."

Derek locked eyes with her and nodded slowly. "He's always been that sweet. He's always been that lost." He smashed his fist against his thigh. "As a kid, he would get upset about the smallest things but always try to take on everyone else's issues while he was dying on the inside."

On the couch, Brent let out a sob. It was clear they'd been through this all before.

"Let me make a phone call," Samantha said.

"He hasn't been missing very long," Derek said. "So, we haven't reached out to the police."

But Samantha worked with the police of Nantucket frequently. They knew her by name, and they knew to trust her. When the secretary at the station answered the phone, she greeted Samantha by name and said, "I hope this is just a pleasantry phone call."

"Unfortunately not," Samantha replied with a sigh. "I was hoping you could tell me something about a very recent missing person. His name is Patrick Elrod, he has addiction issues, and his family is really worried about him."

The secretary was quiet for a moment. "Goodness, yes. The hospital called a few hours ago to report that someone had just dropped him off at the ER and then taken off. We have the make and model of the vehicle, but they didn't catch the plates."

Samantha's heart dropped. "Thank you so much. Do you know if he's okay?"

"I can't tell you more about his medical state," the secretary said. "But I know he was there a couple of hours ago. His family should be able to get more information."

"Thank you. I really appreciate it."

* * *

Samantha drove Derek and Brent to the hospital. Throughout the drive, the brothers were quiet and heavy with worry. Samantha dropped them off at the emergency room waiting area, parked the car, and then hurried inside to find them already in conversation with a nurse at the front desk. Derek nodded firmly as Brent stared straight ahead. Devastation marred his face.

After their talk, Brent disappeared down a hallway, and Derek turned and walked toward Samantha. Samantha was frozen with fear. *Please, don't let him be dead. Please, don't let him be dead.*

"He's stabilized," Derek said. "Thank goodness."

Samantha reached out and grabbed Derek's hand. The act was so easy, so natural. He didn't flinch away.

"He OD'd?" Samantha whispered.

Derek bobbed his head. "Apparently, he's found another crowd around here. Lucky him."

"There are crowds like that everywhere," Samantha said. "On and off the island. If he wants to find them, he will, unfortunately."

"Maybe I should take him to a deserted island," Derek tried. "Maybe I should lock him in his apartment forever, just to make sure he doesn't use."

Samantha had heard similar sentiments before from family members and loved ones of people who dealt with addictions.

"He's sleeping, but he should be awake soon," Derek explained. "The nurse said the doctor will be around shortly to talk. After that, we can see him in his room before visiting hours end for the night." He paused for a moment and locked eyes with her. "You've been such a big help, Samantha. I can't thank you enough." After another pause, he added, "I guess I should take some money off the cost of the redesign."

Samantha rolled her eyes. *How silly to speak of that now.*

"Of course not. We're friends, Derek," she said instead. "I want to be there for you when I can."

Derek looked momentarily surprised as though what she'd said was slightly too earnest. She didn't care. After the heinous date she'd been on only an hour before, she wanted to be upfront with people about her feelings. She didn't want to waste any more time with lies.

For a little while, Derek and Samantha sat on plastic chairs in the waiting room. Brent joined after a while but kept his head down and seemed content to stare at the floor. Samantha knew that everyone mourned in their own way.

After a long silence, Derek spoke. "How are your aunt's diaries?"

"Oh goodness. They've been such an adventure."

"Give me some juicy details to take my mind off this mess," Derek urged.

Samantha knew it was the perfect distraction. She thought for a moment, going over the events of her great-aunt's life back in the sixties and seventies.

"Remember what I said about Jessabelle? That she said she never wanted to get married?"

Derek nodded. "But she'd lied. She had been married to a guy named Arnold."

"Exactly. But I found out why she swore off marriage," Samantha continued. "Apparently, she and her husband really wanted children. Three years passed, and they tried for so long. Still, no children came, and she was heartbroken. She realized her husband no longer looked at her the same way— as though her inability to get pregnant was tied up in how much he could possibly love her. And then, one day, she came home from a beach day with my grandma Margaret, and she caught him cheating."

"No." Derek shook his head.

"It's really sad," Samantha said. "After I read that entry, I looked Arnold up. He wasn't hard to find since he was such a prominent journalist for so many years. Apparently, after his divorce from Jessabelle, he went on to marry the same woman he cheated with."

"Let me guess. They had four beautiful children," Derek said.

"I wish. Actually, they went on to have six!" Samantha explained.

"That must have destroyed your aunt Jessabelle," Derek said.

"She never spoke about this," Samantha reminded him. "As far as I knew, she liked children but had never wanted any herself."

"Listen, I like children. But I never would have wanted that many of them," Derek said with a laugh. But a moment later, his smile was gone. "I can understand why Jessabelle swore off marriage after that. It's the same reason I swore off marriage too."

Samantha's brain was ablaze with this new information. "Did your wife cheat on you?"

Derek nodded. He couldn't make eye contact. "We hadn't been married very long. Three years. I thought she was going on a business trip. Turns out, she was just meeting my best friend in a cabin in the woods."

"Oh gosh. That's awful. I'm so sorry." Samantha wrinkled her nose.

"Pretty bad, yeah. I was lost for several years."

"Did you ever consider dating again?"

"Sure. I've been on dates. But those dating apps are not my cup of tea. No offense if that's what you're into," Derek said.

Samantha's eyes bugged out from her head. "I just went on my first one tonight, actually. It was horrendous! I left before I finished my first glass of wine."

Derek winced. "Impressive."

Samantha felt a beautiful ease as they spoke. It was as though they'd always needed to have this conversation ever since the very first spark. And there *had* been a spark — that was no longer up for debate.

"My husband cheated on me too," Samantha said softly. She felt as though she had opened her ribcage and withdrawn her heart. "In some ways, though, he cheated on me much later than he should have."

"What do you mean?"

"Gosh, it's embarrassing."

Derek shook his head. "I can assure you I won't think anything less of you."

"My husband wasn't exactly kind to me. Every other word out of his mouth was cruel and manipulative. He made me feel as though I was never enough. For a long time, I told myself that was just the way things were. I'm not even sure it bothered me." Samantha's eyes filled with tears, but she quickly blinked them away. "It was only when my girls became old enough to realize how messed up that relationship was that I fully understood what I'd done to myself. I'd built myself a prison. When I told him to leave, to get out, he went to New York City and, apparently, fell in love on the spot." Samantha sputtered with ironic laughter. "They live together now. She's eleven years younger than I am. And I tell myself over and over again that it doesn't matter— that I love my life here. That I wouldn't want anything to change. But the truth is, I hate myself for allowing that relationship to go on for so long. I hate myself for loving him so much. And I'm not sure if I'll ever forgive myself."

Suddenly, Derek's hand was over hers. His eyes were warm, understanding. "None of that sounds like it was your fault."

Samantha closed her eyes. It felt remarkable to hear that, especially coming from a near-stranger. Still, she couldn't believe it.

The doctor appeared behind the desk in the waiting room. The nurse called for Brent and Derek to go back to see their brother. Samantha's heart banged around. She hugged Derek close, then hugged Brent, who looked catatonic.

"Call me later?" Samantha asked.

"Sure," Derek said. He lifted a hand to wave, then disappeared between two white doors.

For a little while, Samantha remained in the waiting room. It was a quiet night. A teenager nursed a broken arm in the corner, his face pale, as his mother reminded him she hadn't wanted to buy the skateboard in the first place. A pregnant woman held a scared-looking child. An older couple sat and held hands in the corner, frequently whispering in one another's ears.

The waiting room was a strange place. Samantha didn't belong there today— this wasn't her tragedy. She stood, her heart in pieces, and walked out of the double-wide doors. Remembering she'd been the one to drive Derek, she quickly texted to tell him she'd come back to take him home. He texted no; they would take a taxi.

On the drive back to the Jessabelle House, Samantha opened all the windows of her car and leaned her head on the seat. She felt at ease at that moment. A million images floated in and out of her head— of Margaret and Jess-abelle, of Derek, Brent, and Patrick, and of her and Daniel as young lovers, up against the world.

They'd all done their best to survive. They'd all failed along the way. That was just what it meant to be alive.

Chapter Thirteen

Understandably, the brothers took a few days off from refurbishing the Jessabelle House. After Patrick's OD, the best route forward was unclear. Samantha sent Derek a number of recommendations for local rehab facilities, along with a promise she would make any phone calls she could to get him into the best location possible. Derek thanked her and said that although Patrick was very weak and coming down from drugs, he seemed grateful to be alive. "He couldn't believe we found him," Derek said on the phone. "I said we had the best help there is."

Without the brothers around the Jessabelle House, Samantha felt very alone. Via text message, she told her daughters she was the new ghost of the bluffs. Her daughters sent rolling eyes emojis and told her to stop being so dramatic. Still, their worry for her brought them over frequently, and they even spent the night a few times. Over wine, they told her the budding drama of the new season, about the boys they thought were cute, and about the difficulties at their jobs. Samantha was sure those conversations couldn't have happened with their father around. Daniel wouldn't have allowed such gossip.

At the end of that heinous week, Samantha met her mother at a little coffee shop in town. When Sam entered, Estelle sat in the corner in her white linen suit and a pair of Chanel sunglasses and wrote in a journal intently. Although Estelle was a popular novelist in some circles, Roland didn't fully respect her career, not that that was a surprise to anyone.

"Mom!" Samantha hugged her mother and inhaled her beautiful perfume.

"Oh, my darling daughter." Estelle smiled as she removed her sunglasses. "I've been lost in this plot all morning long."

"Are you writing a new book?"

Estelle nodded excitedly. "I've been so wrapped up in it that I've nearly forgotten to do everything else. Chores have flown out the window. Your father even had to make his own dinner last night. God bless him."

Samantha wanted to point out that her mother wasn't required to make her husband's dinner every single night of her life, but she kept it to herself.

"I'm guessing he didn't starve?" Samantha asked instead.

Estelle laughed. "He managed to make himself a sandwich."

"Wow. Good for him." Samantha rolled her eyes.

Up at the counter, Samantha and Estelle ordered coffee, soup, and sandwiches. Estelle was spirited, explaining she'd also forgotten to eat much since the new novel had begun to consume her. Samantha adored seeing her mother so energized.

Once at the table, Estelle and Samantha chatted

easily, updating one another on the bits and pieces of their lives. Samantha was careful not to speak too harshly about her father, and Estelle was careful to talk around Roland, saying, "I went here," or, "I did this," instead of "we." Samantha talked about the Jessabelle House and what a pleasure it had been to flesh out a brand-new life in such a gorgeous space. Estelle beamed. "I knew you'd make it your own," she said. "Better than that, Jessabelle knew you'd make it your own. It's why she passed it on to you."

Right before Samantha had to head out for the afternoon, Estelle grabbed her wrist and said, "By the way." There was an urgency in Estelle's voice.

"What is it?"

"I um. I mean, we. Your father and I would like to invite you to a family dinner this Sunday." It seemed difficult for her to say.

Samantha's heart hammered. She couldn't remember the last time she'd been invited to any type of family event, let alone an intimate family supper. *What was going on?* She suspected family dinners were frequent. She could imagine the entire family gathered around that beautiful antique table as Roland, Grant, and Charlie discussed stock prices and real estate. A shiver raced down her spine. *Could she really join them? Did she even want to?*

"It's just that..." Estelle paused. "I think your father has a lot of regrets."

This was bizarre. *Roland Coleman? Filled with regret?* Samantha remembered his large, nostalgic eyes as he'd gazed up at the Jessabelle House on his recent stopover. *What had gotten into him? Was he sick?*

"And we would really love to see Darcy and Rachelle," Estelle added hurriedly. "They're getting so much older now. And who knows if they'll want to stay on the island forever."

Samantha hated when her mother used her daughters as artillery. It almost always worked.

"What time?" Samantha said with a sigh.

* * *

That Sunday at five thirty, Samantha, Darcy, and Rachelle stood on the front porch of the most cursed estate in all of Nantucket Island. Even as they waited for the door to be opened, Samantha's thoughts ran amok with images of teenage Samantha, who'd struggled to survive in such a suffocating environment. In no way had she felt she'd belonged. In no way had she wanted to follow in her father's footsteps and become a proper "Coleman." It had twisted her stomach.

Estelle answered the door with a vibrant "Hello!" Her voice rang through the house. She collected her grand-daughters into her arms and squeezed them, asking how they'd been. Samantha followed in after them, feeling like a stranger.

"I brought wine," Samantha said. She handed her mother a bottle of orange wine, the same one that had come specially recommended by Harry, a man she would never see again.

"Oh goodness. This looks fancy!" Estelle said. "Hilary? Have you had this one before?"

Samantha and her daughters followed Estelle into the living area, where Hilary sat next to her daughter, Ava. Hilary took the bottle of wine and read the label.

"This is really something special," Hilary said, eyeing Samantha. "How did you hear about it?"

Samantha blushed. She wanted to say, *"the most pretentious man I've ever met recommended it to me, so I figured it was perfect for a Coleman party."* Instead, she said, "I've been reading about wine regions."

Hilary was impressed. She stood and hugged Samantha stiffly. Ava did the same. Outside, Charlie, Uncle Grant, and Roland stood together, holding bottles of craft beer. Beyond them, two of Charlie's children, Vince and Sheila, sat in lawn chairs. Vince, who was twenty-six and married to Lucy, had twin babies, who were maybe off somewhere, asleep. Behind Vince, Lucy held a baby monitor in her right hand.

"Wow. It's a full house," Samantha said to Estelle. She was riddled with anxiety. *What had she been thinking?* She'd walked directly into the lion's den. "Can I help you in the kitchen?"

Estelle waved. "I have everything taken care of. You just sit down and catch up with your sister."

Samantha's grin felt fake. She dropped onto the chair across from Ava and Hilary and tried to come up with a single question. Hilary seemed to be doing the same thing.

"So. Rachelle? Darcy?" Hilary turned her attention from Samantha. "Tell me. How is everything? It already feels like summer, doesn't it?"

Rachelle and Darcy nodded dutifully. They spoke about the apartment they shared, then Rachelle took over (bless her heart) and spoke about the restaurant industry on the island. Hilary flinched but asked a decent number of questions. Apparently, she'd been to Rachelle's restaurant before and enjoyed it, although her fish had been too salty.

At that moment, there was a knock on the door.

Samantha fled the living room to get it, grateful to have something to do.

"Oh. Sophie! Jared!" It was Samantha's cousin, Sophie, and her husband, Jared, both of whom were around Samantha's age. For reasons Samantha didn't know, they'd never had children.

"Samantha?" Sophie's smile was bright and welcoming. "I had no idea you would be here!" Suddenly, she hurried to hug her, wrapping her arms around Samantha as though they'd spent their lives as best friends.

Behind Sophie, Jared shifted his weight uncomfortably.

"Um. Hi, Soph!" Samantha chuckled and stepped out of the hug. Sophie continued to wear that big, loose smile. "Can I get you anything?"

"Maybe some wine," Sophie said. "It's a party, isn't it?"

"That's what they're telling me," Samantha said.

Estelle shooed everyone outside, where a large table had been placed beneath two gorgeous oaks. Estelle had decorated it with a white tablecloth and fine china. It was ladened with a pot of clam chowder, roasted Brussels sprouts, asparagus, sweet potatoes, roasted chicken, and freshly baked rolls.

"Everyone, please. Grab a seat," Estelle said.

"This looks incredible, Mom," Charlie complimented. He eyed Samantha as they dropped into chairs around the table, then nodded. "Long time no see, Sam."

"Right back at you," Samantha said. *What does that even mean?* "How is the window and door business going?"

Charlie owned the largest window and door supplier business on the island, which he'd opened in connection with Roland's real estate development business. Most of the doors and windows she and the Elrod brothers had ordered had been via his company. Derek had asked if that was all right, and Samantha had said, "I don't think there's another way." It wasn't that she necessarily liked her brother, but she wouldn't go out of her way not to support him.

"People still need to enter and exit places," Charlie tried to joke. "The door business will never go out of style."

Charlie's wife, Shawna, laughed gently, although Samantha was pretty sure she'd heard that joke four million times before.

Roland sat at the head of the table while Estelle sat at the opposite head. As their children and extended family piled their plates with food, the married couple eyed one another adoringly. Samantha frowned, incredulous. This was the second or third time she'd felt "goodness" from Roland Coleman. *Was she going insane? Or had he just gotten soft in his old age?*

Across the table, Sophie continued to smile. She swayed back and forth in her chair, her eyes alight. Her plate remained empty, as though she'd just forgotten to fill it. She was like a child overstuffed with candy. Beside her, her husband was pale, and his eyes went left and right as though he wanted someone to acknowledge this.

What was going on with Sophie? Samantha had always known her to be much like the other Colemans— rigid, sure of herself, and sure of the rules. *Did anyone else notice how strange she was acting?*

But before Samantha could speak, Roland lifted his glass of wine. His eyes were suddenly focused on her.

"I want to make a toast," he said. "To my daughter,

Samantha, and her two daughters, Rachelle and Darcy. It is an honor to host you here."

Samantha's throat was tight. She raised her glass toward him, conscious that all eyes were upon her.

"And I'd further like to toast your new home, the Jessabelle House," he continued. "What you've done so far to refurbish it is beyond my wildest dreams. I know your great-aunt would be very proud."

Samantha was caught off guard. *Was this Roland's way of making up for being so rude to her a couple of weeks ago? Was it a trap?*

"I would really love to see that old place again," Charlie said. He stabbed his fork through a sweet potato and wielded it over his plate. "Aunt Jessabelle never invited me after I grew up."

"Yeah. Samantha was the only one allowed to go," Hilary said snidely.

Samantha's heart thudded. Jealousy seeped from their words. She wanted to tell them how she'd felt like an outsider amongst them all her life and that Aunt Jessabelle had been her only solace.

Across the table, Sophie closed her eyes, sipped her wine, and continued to sway. If Samantha wasn't mistaken, Sophie was high. Like, really high.

"I would love to see it too," Estelle said kindly. "Perhaps we should all come on the same day. That way, you can get it over with all at once." She winked.

Samantha's mouth felt very dry. She eyed her father, who peered at her kindly. *How could she make an excuse not to invite them over?* It was impossible.

Besides, it seemed that her father wanted to make space for forgiveness. It seemed he wanted to find a way to move on from the horrors of the past. Samantha was an addiction worker— it was her job to ask difficult questions and help other people overcome terrible obstacles. *Why couldn't she use her work strategies within her own family?*

On top of that, her father hadn't mentioned her career or belittled her once since she'd walked through the door. *That was a start, wasn't it?*

Chapter Fourteen

1972

J essabelle was thirty-seven years old and the head librarian in charge of the Nantucket Library. The head office on the third floor looked out over downtown and featured a mahogany desk behind which no woman had ever sat. Every single person in the library had to answer to her, address her as Ms. Oliver, and regard her as a powerful force in the Nantucket academic sector. Even though she didn't have any children and Arnold had left her for another woman and already had a baby, it didn't mean her life wasn't extraordinary.

Recently, Jessabelle discovered that she had a very particular power. Because she no longer wanted to have children or get married, men regarded her as a challenge. She was "difficult" and "different than other women." They chased after her and begged her to love them. But

Jessabelle refused to give her heart to any of them. "My heart will always belong to me," she told them.

Miraculously, it was another solstice. Like always, Jessabelle and Margaret's parents planned to host the party at the house on the bluffs, and like always, Margaret and Jessabelle planned to meet there early to help their mother with hors d'oeuvres.

It was a rare thing to see Margaret at the library. As Jessabelle tied up loose ends with her secretary, Margaret waited in her office and read the first pages of antique books. She looked very pale and thin, as though she no longer saw herself as a part of the living world. Jessabelle had noticed this change as of late, but it was especially apparent now. Because Jessabelle's work was so demanding and Margaret very rarely left the house, Jessabelle hadn't had much time to ask Margaret what was on her mind. Perhaps today was the day.

Jessabelle drove Margaret out to the house on the bluffs. Throughout, Margaret chatted easily about Roland and Grant, about the social committees she belonged to, and about how her neighbor had gotten angry because she'd accidentally trimmed his bush. "I never really knew where the property line was," Margaret explained.

Nothing of what she said was out of the ordinary. Then again, it was also flat and limp. Since Margaret had ended her affair with Trevor nearly two years ago, she no longer burned with the same fire for life.

Once at the house they'd grown up in, Jessabelle and Margaret set themselves up at the kitchen counter and began to prep. Upstairs, their mother vacuumed, and in the living room, their father drank beer and watched television. Neither was listening in.

"Margaret?" Jessabelle started gently. "Are you all right?"

Margaret's face was stiff. "What do you mean?"

Jessabelle raised her eyebrows. "I don't know." What she wanted to say was: *I feel like I've lost my sister. I feel like you're only half the person you once were. I miss you. Without you, my heart is broken.* Instead, she said, "You seem a bit down, a little depressed."

Margaret shrugged. "That's just life, I guess." She continued to roll cookie dough into little balls. Then, she added, "Chuck seems further away from me than ever."

"Has he been away a lot?"

"More than before," Margaret affirmed. "And when he looks at me, it's like he sees all the way through me. I don't know. Ever since I ended things with Trevor and quit my job at the hospital, I've tried my best to be a dutiful, kind, and loving wife. But it's like he wants to make me pay for what I've done."

"Have you told him how you feel?"

Margaret's mouth burst into an ironic smile. "Tell Chuck Coleman how I feel?"

Jessabelle understood. Chuck Coleman wasn't a man of emotional honesty. He was a man of action, pride, and money.

"Have you thought about leaving him?" Jessabelle whispered.

To this, Margaret's jaw dropped. Before she could speak, their mother entered the room to check their work on the hors d'oeuvres and desserts. She squeezed Margaret's shoulder and said, "Wonderful work, darling." She then raised her eyes to Jessabelle. They were frigid. "Jessabelle, I wanted to tell you. Gregory Valentine will be at the party tonight. Like you, he was divorced. And, like you, he never had children. His mother said he'd like to meet you."

"And what is this Gregory Valentine like?" Jessabelle asked. Annoyance rolled over her.

"Like I said. He's about your age, and he never married. What more do you want to know?" her mother asked.

Jessabelle bristled. All at once, she understood why Margaret didn't want to divorce Chuck. Since Arnold had left Jessabelle, their parents had been up in arms, pestering Jessabelle to settle down again. To them, she was incomplete alone. It was just unnatural.

Her career meant nothing to them. It meant nothing to anyone but Jessabelle.

* * *

The guests began to arrive around five thirty. Chuck arrived with Roland and Grant, who were tall and lanky boys of seventeen and nineteen. Already, the world regarded them as men, even if they didn't think of themselves that way. Jessabelle hugged her nephews and teased them gently, making them laugh. She prayed they wouldn't take on too many of their father's personality traits. She prayed they would handle the world softly.

Already, both Roland and Grant had girlfriends. They arrived a little after the boys, both in hippie dresses that showed a little too much leg. Roland introduced his girlfriend as Estelle, and she nearly fell over herself with excitement when she learned Jessabelle was head of the Nantucket Library.

"I want to be a writer someday so badly," she explained. "I want my books to line an entire shelf!"

Jessabelle loved the young woman's enthusiasm. "You can come to the library any time to talk to me about your favorite books."

Estelle blushed and squeezed Roland's hand. "He's a pretty good writer too."

Roland looked embarrassed. "I'm not. It doesn't matter, anyway. You know as well as I do that my father expects me to go into the family business."

Estelle winced. As Roland stepped away to speak to his brother, she said, "I keep telling Roland he should do whatever he wants."

"The Coleman family is very focused on image," Jessabelle whispered. "I can't imagine he sees any other way forward."

Estelle looked very sad for a moment, too sad for her age. But soon after, Grant's girlfriend, Katrina, came to fetch her, saying she had to join their game. Jessabelle waved her off, then turned to grab herself a glass of wine from the long table on the veranda. Around her, the party widened and intensified to a loud hum, like many crickets all together in the woods.

To Jessabelle's surprise, when she turned back from the drink table, a man she hadn't seen in quite some time entered the party. It was Doctor Trevor Rushford. Beside him was a beautiful woman several years younger than Jessabelle, perhaps even in her twenties. His smile was dapper and arrogant.

Jessabelle hurried to Margaret, who hadn't noticed him yet. "Hi! Can I talk to you inside?"

Once inside, Jessabelle explained who she'd seen. All the color drained from Margaret's face. "I can't believe he'd show his face here."

"Does anyone else know about the affair?" Jessabelle said quietly.

Margaret shook her head. "Not that I know of. Gosh, he's just coming here to rub this in my face. He was so angry when I ended things." She closed her eyes. "I've been thinking lately that every man in the world is allowed buckets of happiness while every woman in the world gets the scraps."

Jessabelle hugged her sister, suddenly red with anger. She couldn't let Dr. Trevor Rushford get away with this. "I'll take care of it."

Jessabelle pressed through the crowd with her wine-glass lifted. When she finally found Trevor, he was holding court in front of three of Jessabelle's family members and several women she didn't know. Everyone gazed at him, impressed with the successful doctor and his stories.

"So, I asked the nurse, I said, 'Nurse? Have we lost him?' Because I was pretty sure I'd just heard the patient flatline. But suddenly, the patient popped up from the table, looked me in the eye, and asked me, 'Does that come with French fries?'"

Everyone howled with laughter. There was no way to tell if Trevor's anecdotes were true. The medical field was a mysterious one.

Suddenly, Jessabelle placed her hand on his upper arm. He flinched and turned to look at her. His eyes told her he knew exactly who she was.

"Hello, Trevor. Can I have a word?" Jessabelle asked.

As Jessabelle led Trevor away from the crowd, she searched her mind for a plan. *What could she tell this man to get him to leave?* But as they headed to the outskirts of the crowd, Chuck spotted them. As Chuck's scowl grew more monstrous, Jessabelle's heart dropped into her stomach. *How could she protect her sister from these horrible men?*

"Listen," Jessabelle said to Trevor under her breath. "I don't know what kind of game you think you're playing. This is Margaret's real life. This is her father's house. That is her husband over there, and those are her children. Now, unless you want Chuck to break your nose, I suggest you leave this instant."

To this, Trevor sneered. He bent low to make eye contact with her. "Do you think for a second that man treats her the way she's supposed to be treated?"

"Their marriage is none of your concern," Jessabelle countered.

"I give it three years before he leaves her for someone prettier and younger," Trevor snarled. "Mark my words."

"I don't care what your silly prediction is," Jessabelle hissed. "I just need you to get off my family's property before I get my daddy's shotgun from under his bed and make you leave."

Still wearing that horrible smile, Trevor lifted his palms to the sky and began to back toward the line of cars in the driveway. "I like how sassy you are, Jessabelle. Call me when you want to have a good time."

Jessabelle glowered at him until he finally turned on his heel and walked the rest of the way toward his car. The young woman he'd brought with him scampered after him like an abandoned pet.

Hours later, the party had reached a state of disarray. Fireworks exploded over the Nantucket Sound. The wine was refilled at random as beers were cracked. Nobody kept track of how much they drank anymore— it was no use. Unlike the others, Jessabelle was mostly sober, and she wandered through the crowd, alternating between disgust and amusement. Her father and mother held one another and swayed beneath the moonlight, still championing a love they'd agreed to so many decades before. Good for them.

Suddenly, Chuck appeared before her. He was sweaty and wet-eyed, and he gripped Jessabelle's shoulders and seethed. "What was he doing here? What were you saying to him?"

The intensity caught Jessabelle off guard. She glanced around, searching for Margaret, but couldn't find her.

"I love her, you know," Chuck blabbered. "Your sister. I love her. All I wanted in the world was to build a life with her."

Jessabelle was at a loss. Under her breath, she said, "Then why can't you treat her like you love her?"

Chuck staggered back, surprised. It was as though Jessabelle had pierced him with a knife.

"Just grow up. Be a man. And talk to her," Jessabelle continued. "Most of the problems in this crazy world can be solved with a conversation."

With that, Jessabelle tore through the crowd, entered the house, grabbed her things, and fled. She'd had enough of this silly solstice party. She was finished with people's crazy behavior. Only when she was settled in bed with a book could she breathe properly again.

Chapter Fifteen

Present Day

The day after the Coleman family dinner party, Samantha agreed to meet Derek at Patrick's apartment. Since Patrick had been released from the hospital, he'd spent days in heavy withdrawal, and Derek and Brent had taken turns caring for him. The pain of withdrawal was an excruciating thing to witness— and those undergoing it were not always the kindest or the easiest to be around. As it had been several days by then, Samantha was sure Patrick was through the worst of it.

Derek opened the door of Patrick's apartment with shell-shocked eyes. Without waiting a moment, he hugged Samantha close and said, "Thank you for coming. This means so much to us."

The first thing Samantha noticed was the smell of the apartment. It was a putrid smell that assaulted her nostrils all at once. The cleaning solution on the counter told her Derek and Brent had tried their best to cover it up.

"He just woke up," Derek explained. "I think he had a rough night."

"Does it seem to be getting better?"

Derek shrugged. "Maybe? I don't know. Brent and I are both so exhausted. I don't know if we fully register what's going on."

"And he's up to having a talk?"

"I think so," Derek said. "He trusts you."

Samantha waited nervously with a cup of tea. Although she'd had these sorts of talks with her clients too many times to count at this point, this incident was different. It was personal. The brothers were her friends, and Patrick was dear to her. Beyond that, the ongoing intensity between her and Derek made her feel like they were at the beginning of something— something that could become beautiful. She didn't want to make a wrong move now that would destroy the potential for that future.

Patrick emerged from the bathroom a few minutes later. He'd showered, and his hair was slick across his forehead. His eyes were still slightly empty, and he was very skinny and weak. When he collapsed on the chair beside her, he rubbed his temples. The living room was very quiet.

"I guess you're used to seeing people in my kind of shape, huh?" Patrick said.

Samantha needed to be professional to instate her authority. It was the only way.

"I'm not sure I explained my qualifications when we met, Patrick, but yes. I'm a qualified addiction worker with a great deal of experience in the field. In my tenure, I've dealt with hundreds of people with addictions— people from all walks of life and all states of income. Furthermore, I have numerous relationships with rehab facilities across the state of Massachusetts and beyond, and I genuinely believe in the power of those facilities. I've seen many people get better, build stable and normal lives, and flourish."

Patrick nodded and furrowed his brow. He did not seem to want to believe her.

Samantha softened her tone. "How are you feeling, Patrick?"

Patrick coughed. "Like garbage."

"I imagine so. Withdrawal is a horrible thing."

"It's my sixth time," Patrick confessed. "Sixth full withdrawal. Sixth time getting sober. I'm beginning to think it's impossible."

"It isn't, Patrick. And more than that, it's important to change that narrative in your own mind. Getting sober is possible. It's possible in every case, but it's up to you and no one else. You have to find your purpose."

Even as Samantha said this, she was reminded of the real statistics— that the more times people relapsed, the less likely it was they could ever get clean. Still, Patrick had to try. There was no other way.

There was something amiss about the apartment around them. The leather couch was drab, the walls were gray, and the stench seemed to contain no oxygen. Had Samantha been living there, she wouldn't have had any hope for her sobriety, either.

Suddenly, she heard herself say the impossible.

"I don't normally do this," she began. "But would you like to come stay with me for a little while? Just until you fully withdraw. I have plenty of guest rooms, and the air and the water and the sun can only do you good. While you're there, we can discuss logistics, like the next steps and rehab. But until then, you can relax somewhere a bit more comfortable."

Patrick looked at her like a deer in headlights.

Derek sputtered. "You really don't have to do that."

But already, Samantha sensed it was the right thing. Patrick's hollow eyes were terrifying— a reminder that if he didn't give up on drugs soon, he would ultimately overdose again and lose at this game he was playing. Samantha couldn't allow that to happen.

"It won't be forever. Just for a little while," Samantha urged them. "Enough of the house is finished up. We'll be comfortable. Besides, I'm pretty lonely there all by myself."

Finally, Patrick began to nod. He locked eyes with Derek, then shrugged and said, "Why the heck not?"

Within the next fifteen minutes, Derek had packed Patrick a bag. Together, Samantha and Derek helped Patrick from the apartment and into Derek's car, where Patrick laid himself down in the back and stared at the roof. With the door closed, Derek whispered to Samantha, "I don't even know what to say."

"Say you'll stay with us," Samantha insisted .

Derek's eyes widened. After a brief moment of stuttering, he said, "Okay. Okay!" Then, he hurried to the driver's side. "I'll meet you there?"

At the Jessabelle House, Samantha stretched sheets over the bed in the third guest room, the one she hadn't given to either Rachelle or Darcy. Patrick followed her in as she pulled a pillowcase over a pillow, then sat on the bed. Exhaustion made his shoulders fall forward.

"It really is such a stunning house," he said. "Beyond

my wildest dreams to even work at a place like this, let alone stay."

Samantha placed the pillow gently at the head of the bed. Patrick's eyes followed it hungrily. Clearly, he was ready to pass out again.

"You'll tell me if you need anything at all?" Samantha asked, cocking an eyebrow.

Patrick nodded sleepily and fell back onto the bed. Samantha tip-toed from the room and closed the door behind her, confident that Patrick had already fallen into a haze.

Samantha found Derek on the veranda. He had his face in his hands, and his eyes were elsewhere, lost in thought.

"I think he fell back asleep," Samantha reported as she sat next to him.

"That's a relief."

Samantha placed a hand on Derek's shoulder and rubbed it tenderly. Derek's muscles relaxed slightly.

"He said he's relapsed six times after sobriety," Derek said softly. "I've only been around for three of them. Each time feels worse than the last."

"I take it this started when you were teenagers?"

Derek nodded. "It's not that Brent and I were always clean. We drank a little too much. Sometimes, we took a little something if it was around. But Patrick always took everything to an extreme. It was like he couldn't stop himself."

"He definitely *couldn't* stop himself," Samantha corrected. "He's an addict. It's a disease. Nothing he can help."

"Right. I know that. Just at the time, we didn't understand that at all. And our dad noticed something was wrong pretty early on. Gosh, he used to scream at Patrick like nothing else. He told him he was worthless, that he wasn't good enough to be his son. One time, when he said that, I screamed at our father and told him he didn't mean that. But Dad said, 'Yes, I do. I mean that.' And then, he stormed off, and Patrick left the house to go use.

"I don't know why my dad was always so angry," Derek added. "I'm sure he had trauma from his own father, who I never knew. I know these things are passed down from generation to generation. I know that history repeats itself."

Samantha bobbed her head up and down, having thought similar thoughts recently about her own family.

"When I married my ex-wife, we talked about having kids for a while," Derek continued. "But I kept having nightmares. In some of the nightmares, I was like my father. I screamed at our children. I told them how stupid they were and how unlucky I'd been to have them. In other nightmares, my son was just like Patrick— always using, always destroying himself.

"Eventually, the nightmares were so overbearing that I stopped having sex and being affectionate with my wife. I didn't want children, not in the slightest, because I was terrified of what would happen to them." Derek turned to show red-rimmed eyes. "I shouldn't blame her for cheating on me. I had no love to give her. I was a mess wrapped up in fear and anger."

In the silence that followed, Samantha felt her body fall forward. She wrapped her arms around Derek and closed her eyes as he shivered against her. The pain and regret from the past remained around them, always eager to tear them back to their depths.

That night, Samantha ordered pizza and opened a

bottle of wine. It was only a Monday, but Derek and Samantha sipped two glasses, ate melted cheese and bread, and watched the sun fall into the water. Once, Patrick appeared on the veranda with a glass of water, and he smiled at the two of them, grateful to be in their company and to feel the last of the sun on his face.

That night, Samantha and Derek cleaned the plates and put the rest of the pizza in the fridge. It was nearly ten, and Samantha had begun to suppress her yawns.

"By the way," Derek said as he dried a plate with a hand towel. "How are the diaries going?"

Samantha laughed with surprise. "You're genuinely curious about this, aren't you?"

"I think it's just nice to learn about family drama that isn't my own," Derek admitted.

"I can understand that." Samantha sipped her wine. "As Jessabelle gets older in the diaries, I'm getting a better picture of the tragedy of my grandma Margaret's life," Samantha said. "She already died so young. I mean, fifty-one is only six years away from my current age! And before that, it sounds like she struggled with knowing what she wanted."

"Welcome to the club," Derek said.

"I know. It's true. It's a worldwide problem. It sounds like my grandpa Chuck really loved my grandmother and vice versa. But neither of them knew how to talk to each other."

Derek winced. "That hits a little close to home."

"Yes." Samantha shook her head. "Daniel and I had terrible communication. I just did whatever he said all the time because it seemed easier that way."

Derek grimaced . "That doesn't sound like the way you are now."

"Thanks for saying that," Samantha said. "I'm trying to overcome my people-pleasing habits and really tune into who I am. I just hate that it took forty-five years to get to that point." Samantha headed to the bookcase and pulled out the most recent diary she'd been reading, taken from a later year. "Do you want to read a bit before we go to bed?"

"Together?" Derek asked.

"If it isn't too boring for you," Samantha said.

Derek's smile was enormous. "I can't think of anything else I'd rather do."

Chapter Sixteen

1982

Jessabelle was now forty-seven years old and, in some circles, probably regarded as an "old maid." Given her success at the Nantucket Library and her general contentment with her life so far, she wasn't sure she cared what anybody thought. This was the greatest gift of all— freedom from public opinion. She wished she could give it as a gift to her sister, who struggled continually with fears surrounding what everyone thought of her. She was especially worried about public opinion regarding her marriage to Chuck. Although Margaret hadn't cheated on Chuck in over ten years, guilt tore through her, and she was suspicious of everyone. "Do you think someone knows what I did?" she asked Jessabelle every few months, panic in her eyes.

This deep in middle age, the Oliver sisters hadn't managed to avoid the horrible sorrow that was inevitable with the passage of time. Within the previous three years, they'd lost both of their parents. Their mother had died suddenly in a car accident, and their father had died two years after that, presumably of a broken heart. Both Margaret and Jessabelle continued to mourn them. They brought them up in daily conversations in an attempt to keep them alive in small ways, cooked their mother's old recipes, and quoted their father's silly anecdotes. Still, Jessabelle was certain she would find herself on her knees with sadness about their death at odd times for the rest of her life. It was something she would never fully get over.

Jessabelle's father had left their home on the bluffs to her in his will, calling it, in official documentation, the "Jessabelle House." This had come as a huge surprise to Jessabelle, as she'd always suspected that her parents hadn't liked her as much as they'd liked Margaret. She'd never given them grandchildren, she'd dated around and created gossip across the island, and she'd focused on her career rather than family values. When the executor of her father's estate had handed the keys over, she'd been flabbergasted. And then, when she'd stepped into the house and regarded it as her own for the first time, she'd pressed her face into her father's jacket and cried on the bed her father and mother had shared. Unable to handle her own emotions, she'd spent the first few months in her childhood bedroom, half pretending her parents would return home at any moment to claim theirs.

All she'd wanted in the world was to be a little girl again— to play in the sands with Margaret and hold her parents' hands. She could never get any of that time back. It was permanently gone.

It was June, and Jessabelle wore button-up summer dresses and wandered the beaches and hills with her heart on her sleeve and a taste of adventure and goodwill. Across the horizon, sailboats opened their sails to a beautiful and brand-new summer. For dinner, she cooked herself nutritional meals— fish, spinach, and chicken— and she found that her muscles were spry and youthful, as though she was back in her twenties again. But now that she was forty-seven, she wouldn't have liked to be in her twenties again. What a heinous time of confusion that had been! The pressure to marry had consumer her every waking moment. It had taken over her mind and practically possessed her.

Now and then, Jessabelle heard about Arnold through the grapevine. An academic, he'd wanted his children in the very best schools in New England, and he'd moved his large family to Boston. In the previous twelve years, he and his second wife had graced the world with three more children. Rumor had it they weren't done yet.

After an invigorating walk along the sands, Jessabelle returned home to find her sister on the veranda. She had her bare feet propped up on the railing, and she'd unbuttoned her dress to reveal a bikini beneath.

"I would never wear a bikini in front of anyone but you these days," Margaret said as Jessabelle mounted the steps. "I hope it isn't too offensive."

Jessabelle rolled her eyes and kissed her sister on the forehead. Before Margaret could say another word, she stripped to her bikini and lay beside her. The sun beat upon them like a benediction.

"I can't believe it's another solstice party," Margaret commented. "Are you sure you're up for this?"

Jessabelle laughed. "Are you suggesting I call the party off five hours before it's set to begin? Mother would kill me."

In the kitchen, Jessabelle and Margaret performed the ordinary rituals called for before the solstice party. They sliced vegetables, baked cookies, made spinach tarts, and placed hot dogs wrapped in croissant dough on sticks. Throughout, they sipped lemonade and a tiny bit of white wine to get them in the mood for the party. They also discussed the guest list, which was just as long as it had ever been when their parents had been alive, if not longer.

"What ever happened to Dr. Trevor?" Jessabelle asked out of the blue as she lifted the spinach tarts from the oven. For some reason, he'd been on her mind lately.

Margaret grimaced. "He got married and moved away."

Jessabelle eyed Margaret, looking for some sign of sorrow or regret. Margaret's face was difficult to read.

"I'm sure, as a husband, he's the same as Chuck. He's probably always at the hospital, always on-call. I'm sure his wife, whoever she is, feels just as lonely as I do some nights." Margaret poured herself another glass of lemonade and gazed out the window. "Everything happens for a reason," she finished, as though that was all that needed to be said.

Just like always, the guests for the solstice party began to arrive around five thirty. Jessabelle, the hostess, did her best to make the rounds, compliment dresses, pass out beers, and point to the food table. Her face ached from smiling too much. Several librarians she worked with at the Nantucket Library arrived, grinning meekly, as though they hadn't spent much time outside the walls of the library and weren't sure how to socialize. Jessabelle pushed them into the crowd, eager to see what would happen.

Chuck arrived not long after that. At forty-eight, he was more handsome than ever, and his swagger as he roamed the party turned Jessabelle's stomach. She watched as he kissed Margaret's cheek and spoke to her quietly. *What did they say to each other when no one was around?* Jessabelle knew that all marriages were heavy with secrets— that to let those secrets free was similar to polluting the marriage.

Roland and Grant were now twenty-seven and twenty-nine years old and spitting images of their father. Of the two, Grant was the golden child, as he'd followed in his father's footsteps and ultimately broadened Chuck's kingdom and wealth.

Roland had decided not to go into trading. Rather, he'd announced at the tender age of twenty-one that he wanted to go out on his own as a real estate developer. "The real estate across Nantucket and Martha's Vineyard is booming right now. I want to get on the ground floor," Jessabelle had heard him say. Behind his words, she'd heard a man much like Chuck Coleman himself— an arrogant man who felt he deserved the world.

Then again, Roland's decision had been a shrewd one. Very soon, his wealth had doubled and then tripled in size.

"Hi, Aunt Jessabelle!" Roland greeted her and kissed her on the cheek. Beside him was his beautiful wife, Estelle, who'd joined the Coleman family at a very young age. Although the wedding ceremony had been beautiful, Jessabelle had ached with worry for her, praying that she'd made the right choice for her life, career, and happiness.

Now, Estelle carried their youngest, her three-year-old daughter named Hilary. Her middle child, Samantha, hid behind her leg as their eldest, Charlie, ran through the grass near the veranda, howling with the other children. Pregnancy had been second nature for her.

"You have a beautiful family," Jessabelle told Estelle warmly. "Can I get you anything?"

Estelle blushed. "It's strange to have someone offer me something for a change."

"I imagine you have your hands full. Three children! I hope you still find time to write?"

"Not as much as I'd like, I'm afraid." Estelle grimaced. "But once they get a little bit older, I plan to carve out that time for myself again."

Jessabelle placed her hand on Estelle's shoulder. "You must. Unlike so many people, you've found something that sets your soul on fire. You cannot let it go."

Jessabelle hurried in and out of the house, grabbing more hors d'oeuvres, refilling the punch, and pausing for hellos and small talk. Her shins were on fire. Margaret chased after her, running herself ragged as she picked up the slack.

Once at the drink table, Jessabelle turned to catch sight of Chuck hovering with a cigar near the bushes. His face was very pale, almost stricken. Next to him, Roland spoke with his hands. His motions were aggressive and charged with adrenaline. It was clear that father and son were in the middle of a massive fight. *But what on earth could they be fighting about? They weren't in business together.*

Did Roland and Chuck just not get along? Maybe Margaret had kept that from Jessabelle. Oh, what a tragedy to hate members of your immediate family. She pondered whether or not she could ask Margaret about the exchange later. Perhaps pointing it out would only make Margaret upset. She'd given everything to her family— and she'd been left alone and loveless, her son angry with his father, and her career dried to dust.

Midway through the party, Margaret and Jessabelle paused in the kitchen to drink glasses of water. Jessabelle kept the story of Roland and Chuck's fight to herself.

"I had no idea how much work this was for Mother and Father," Jessabelle breathed between gulps.

"Mother usually slept for a full day afterward," Margaret reminded her.

Suddenly, there was a horrible smash against the side of the house. Jessabelle and Margaret locked eyes with concern before bursting down the hallway toward the sound. Soon, they found themselves in their father's old study, where Jessabelle had accidentally left a window open.

"Oh my gosh!" Margaret cried and smacked her hand over her mouth.

There on their father's desk perched a bluebird. He looked at them curiously and tilted his head. Still, he seemed authoritative and sharp, as though he'd belonged in the study all this time.

"Do you think he's injured?" Jessabelle asked. The smash hadn't sounded healthy.

"I don't know..." Margaret took a delicate step forward. To this, the bluebird jumped back but still didn't fly away. "He's obviously frightened."

Jessabelle closed the door behind her to ensure the bird wouldn't fly through the rest of the house. With this barrier between them and the rest of the party, relief flooded through her.

"Maybe we should take a moment in here," she suggested.

Margaret chuckled. "Your guests would miss you."

Jessabelle walked daintily to the corner of the room to get a different angle on the bird. "I don't see anything wrong with his wings, but I'm no expert."

"I wonder what he thought he would find if he flew in here," Margaret said.

"Aren't bluebirds supposed to be mean?"

"I think that's blue jays," Margaret corrected.

"Do you think it's a sign of something?" Jessabelle asked. "Should we be worried?"

They were quiet for a moment. The bluebird's black eyes sparkled. A calm overtook the room and made it easier for the three of them to breathe.

But all at once, a storm came down the hallway. Footsteps pounded, and male voices carried. There was a frenetic energy outside the door. Jessabelle almost cried out to tell whoever it was not to come into the study. Before she could, the men were right outside the door, where they lowered their voices. Still, their harsh whispers carried beneath the crack.

"What's gotten into you?" It was Grant. "You've acted like a mad man all evening."

Roland's voice came next. "I hate him, Grant. I hate him so much."

"Are you going to drop hints all night long? Or are you going to tell me what's up?" Grant was exasperated.

In the study, Margaret walked slowly toward the door. Jessabelle's instinct was the grab her, to hold her back from whatever this was. But the two of them were trapped in that study— as Grant and Roland muttered secrets Margaret and Jessabelle should never have known.

"I mean, come on. Think about Dad. Think about

Dad's life. Haven't we seen signs to doubt how trust-worthy he is?" Roland demanded.

"What are you talking about? He's a hard worker," Grant countered. "He's built a beautiful life for us here. I mean, he's one of the most respected businessmen in all of Nantucket."

"Listen to yourself! You've drunk his Kool-Aid," Roland shot back.

"You can't accuse me of not knowing something that I can't possibly know," Grant returned.

Margaret wavered on her feet. Jessabelle stepped forward, wanting to be a pillar of strength. Wherever this conversation was headed, it didn't sound good.

"All those weekends away. Entire months, sometimes. I mean, it's so obvious, isn't it?"

"What's so obvious, Roland?"

"He's been having an affair!" Roland rasped.

"What? He wouldn't. He's a family man. He puts us first," Grant refuted.

"You sound delusional," Roland returned angrily.

"And? How do you know this for sure?"

"I saw him with my own two eyes. Last month, I went to Martha's Vineyard for my new build. It was an exten-sive project, and I stayed on the island for a few nights to ensure it started on the right foot. One night, I went out with a few of my colleagues for dinner. We entered a restaurant in downtown Oak Bluffs, and there he was."

"So?" Grant demanded.

"He sat with a woman and two little girls," Roland continued. "There he was, Mr. Family Man, slicing the chicken of the youngest of the two. Beside him, this woman had these ridiculous goo-goo eyes. She looked at him as though he was everything she could ever want.

And as I approached the table to accost him, the older little girl called him..."

Roland stuttered with sorrow.

"What?" Grant questioned in disbelief. "What did she call him?"

"She called him 'daddy.'"

There was silence on the other side of the door. Beside Jessabelle, Margaret's face was marred with pain as tears rolled down her cheeks. She stood there, frozen in her spot.

"Was she confused?" Grant asked .

"No!" Roland was obstinate. "When Dad saw me coming toward him at the table, he looked like a criminal who'd just been caught red-handed. Before I could explode in the restaurant, he grabbed my elbow and hurried me outside. I felt like a little kid again, like my father wanted to reprimand me. But before he could speak, I screamed at him, demanding what was going on. He was very quiet until I calmed down, which I thought was strange. Over here on Nantucket, he's always so quick to bite. He just explodes. You remember how he was with Mom over the years— always tearing her to shreds. But there on Martha's Vineyard, it was like he didn't want to upset the little girls in the restaurant. This made me even angrier."

"What did he say?" Grant whispered.

"He said there are a lot of things about his life that I can't possibly understand," Roland muttered. "Which I find ridiculous. I asked him who those people were at the table— who was he spending all this time with? And he told me..." Roland stuttered. "He told me the woman was named Mia and that he was in love with her. And that the two little girls were their children, Oriana and Meghan."

Unsure what else to do, Jessabelle rushed for Margaret and wrapped her arms around her. She placed her hand around Margaret's head and clung to her tightly. Around them, the world spun off its axis and throttled into outer space. Around them, everything changed forever.

"What are we going to do?" Grant murmured , on the verge of tears. "I mean, what's stopping us from going out there and telling Mom about all of this right now?"

"I don't know," Roland said. "But Dad wants to have a meeting with us tomorrow night to talk about it."

"Talk about it? You really want to talk about it with him?" Grant demanded. "I mean, what else is there to say?"

"I want more answers," Roland mumbled . "I want explanations. But more than that, I want to make it clear to him that my relationship with him is now over. He's betrayed us. He's betrayed, Mom. And after our talk tomorrow, he's as good as dead to me."

Not long after, Roland and Grant returned to the party and left Margaret and Jessabelle in the study. They were quiet for what seemed like twenty minutes, perhaps half an hour. When Margaret finally wiggled out of Jessabelle's hug to breathe better, she turned too quickly and frightened the bluebird. It spread its wings abruptly and surged toward the window, where it clipped its right wing and flew sideways toward the sky. Together, the Oliver sisters watched as the injured bird flew crookedly, knowing that very soon, it would fall from the sky and to its death.

Chapter Seventeen

Present Day

Patrick and Derek had been living at the Jessabelle House for over a week. Together, the three of them had created a manageable schedule, one with breakfasts and dinners together, walks along the water, and good nights of sleep, which healed them more than they knew. Patrick's eyes had a light to them, and Derek was hopeful that he'd come away from the darkness for good. But Samantha wasn't so sure. Patrick needed real treatment. He needed to go away for a little while and slay his demons before he could face his life again.

Recently, Samantha and Derek had read passages from Jessabelle's diary together and discovered an enormous family secret, one that split Samantha in two. Since that night, she and Derek had hardly spoken about it. It was as though Derek sensed the topic was so intense for her that she wasn't ready to have a full discussion.

Still, it was strange to know that Derek carried Samantha's secret around with him, protecting it. It was strange, too, that Samantha already trusted him so deeply. When Samantha found the strength to comprehend the weight of the past, she knew Derek would be right there beside her, steadying her.

It was morning in mid-June, and light cascaded across the veranda. Samantha walked toward the outdoor table with a big pot of coffee, her hair still slightly wet from her shower. Derek and Patrick ate eggs and sausages and chatted quietly. When Samantha refilled Patrick's mug, he said, "I think we should keep working on the house."

Samantha stalled. "I don't know if that's a good idea." She didn't want to push Patrick into any kind of stress.

"Derek just told me you're hosting a big family party," Patrick said. "Don't you want the place to look as good as possible before then?"

"Oh, I don't care," Samantha lied. In truth, a part of her wanted to show just how "worthy" she was of the Coleman family. Only when she had their respect could she decide if she even wanted it.

"Okay. If not for your family, for you," Derek insisted. "Besides, when you leave for work every day, Patrick and I just wander around the beach and eat snacks. We're bored."

Patrick nodded, his eyes twinkling. Samantha knew this wasn't entirely true, though. Derek told her that he, Patrick, and Brent had been having deep, soul-searching conversations about their childhood trauma, about Patrick's addiction, and how Patrick's addiction had affected all of them. Samantha had urged Derek to do this — it was a first step toward healing.

"That reminds me. I have to pick up more of those snacks you like," Samantha teased. "I never imagined a grown man could go through so many oatmeal cream pies."

Patrick grimaced, trying to tease her. "You have something bad to say about my oatmeal cream pies?"

Derek and Samantha burst into laughter.

"I would never diss your one true love," Samantha joked.

After another pause, Derek sipped his coffee and caught her eye. "The rest of the handiwork is obviously no charge."

"That's unnecessary," Samantha said. "It's your livelihood."

But Derek and Patrick wouldn't hear of it.

"I have all the tools we need in the van in the driveway," Derek asserted . "Brent says he can be here within the hour. Your party's on the twenty-first, right? That means we can finish up the downstairs study and the extra bathroom and then really fine-tune the exterior, all in time for that big, overwhelming family of yours to come over and see it."

Samantha sighed. She could see there was no talking them out of it. "Okay. But I need you both to promise me you'll take breaks when you need to, that you'll drink plenty of fluids, and that you'll stop at midday when the sun gets too hot."

Patrick and Derek both agreed to her terms. Samantha had the strangest instinct to lean down and kiss Derek on the lips as she paraded from the veranda out to her car. It was another busy day of work on Nantucket

Island— and an early-morning meeting with Kenny and Connie awaited her. Kenny had just returned from rehab and managed to get his job back. It was Samantha's job to assess his current emotional state. It was her job to guide him through this next phase post-rehab when he was expected to stay sober on his own. It wasn't easy.

* * *

That afternoon, Samantha met Rachelle and Darcy for a rare lunch. They met at the coffee shop and ordered various juices and sandwiches. As they sat in the shade outside the coffee shop, Rachelle showed off a horrible cut on her finger from last night's restaurant chaos.

"You look proud of it," Darcy accused Rachelle, wrinkling her nose.

Rachelle laughed. "It's the mark of a chef, I guess. Then again, I worry it makes me look like I don't know what I'm doing or unorganized."

"Everyone makes mistakes," Samantha said. "Even that demanding boss of yours."

"I don't know. He's more of a machine than a man," Rachelle explained.

Although Samantha didn't get into the specifics of Patrick's current status, she did mention that the brothers had restarted their work on the Jessabelle House. "They want to finish it in time for this silly party I've agreed to host."

Rachelle wrinkled her nose. "Are you really sure you want to do this?"

"I mean, it sounds like they're jealous you got the Jessabelle House," Darcy pointed out. "Maybe they're up to something."

"But legally, it's yours, right?" Rachelle asked. "They can't take it away from you somehow?"

Samantha's heart thudded. Although she'd never explicitly put a wedge between her daughters and the rest of the Colemans, she had explained the dynamics between herself and her father. He hadn't wanted her to chase her dreams or cared about her individuality. He'd only wanted her to be an extension of himself— a powerful Coleman following in his footsteps like the rest of his children, to carry on his legacy.

"I don't think there's any way they can take the house away from me," Samantha assured her daughters. "Besides, wasn't your grandfather a little softer around the edges at dinner last week? Didn't he seem, I don't know, more open?"

Rachelle and Darcy exchanged doubtful glances. Probably, they'd seen Samantha's weakness with Daniel and extended it to everything else. Daniel had hurt her, even belittled her. For this reason, he and any other man like him were her daughters' biggest enemies.

"Listen. If you really want to do this, you're going to want an impressive array of snacks," Rachelle said finally.

Darcy clapped. "Oh my goodness! Yes. Rachelle, can I be your sous chef?"

"I'll put you to work. Don't worry about that."

Samantha's heart lifted. As Rachelle began to brainstorm potential hors d'oeuvres for the big night, Samantha nibbled her sandwich and watched the tourists mill through downtown, the women in pretty dresses and the men in boat shoes. For not the first time since she'd read the 1982 diary entries that had divulged her grandfather's deepest, darkest secrets, she swayed with fear and worry. *Could any of it be true? Had Grandpa Chuck really had a second family on Martha's Vineyard? And how had Margaret managed to move on after learning of this through the study door on the evening of the* solstice party? She'd heard it from her sons, no less.

It had surely been the most painful thing in Margaret's life. She'd given up on her lover, Trevor, only to be cast into another world of doubt and betrayal.

"Mom?" Rachelle waved a hand over Samantha's face.

"Earth to Mom!" Darcy laughed. "What do you think? Margaritas at the solstice party?"

"Oh. Sure, that's a great idea." Samantha rubbed her temples. "I'll need one or two to deal with the Colemans, that's for sure."

When Samantha returned home that night, she found Derek at the top of a ladder, installing the last of the new shutters to the exterior of the old Victorian. Patrick held the ladder beneath him, watching his every move from below. Samantha carried groceries into the kitchen, where she found Brent with a glass of water. His face was covered in grime.

"What happened?" She was stricken.

Brent waved. "Nothing to worry about. I took a stupid tumble from the ladder. My brothers reprimanded me enough for one day."

"So, I can reprimand you tomorrow?" Samantha winced and searched her cabinets for Tylenol.

"It's not that bad. It just looks worse than what it is," he explained. He sipped his water, then added, "We got even more work done today than we expected to."

Samantha grimaced. "I really didn't want you guys to go back to work already. I know it's been a difficult time."

"The thing is, we spent so many years apart," Brent

explained. "Being here together, fixing up your house...
it's been extraordinary for us. I feel like we're closer than
ever. Yes, Patrick relapsed recently, and yes, that broke
Derek and I's hearts. But then again, we've been here to
help him every step of the way, unlike so many other
times. And besides." He palmed his neck. "I mean, you're
a factor we haven't had before. Patrick respects you. More
than that, he likes you. And I think with your guidance, it
might really stick this time."

Samantha smiled sadly. She'd heard similar sentiments from so many family members. "I'm here for you,
whatever you need."

"We know," Brent told her. "And we can't thank you
enough."

Several hours later, after Brent had returned home
and Patrick had retreated to his bedroom, Samantha and
Derek wandered to the beach to walk barefoot in the
sand. The moon hung low and cast its light across the
cascading waves. For a long time, they remained wordless,
lost in the drama of the dark beach.

Samantha heard herself speak. "I think it's wonderful
you and your brothers have begun to say the things you
always wanted to say. I mean, we only have this one life,
right? It shouldn't give us time to harbor secrets. We
should be telling everyone how we feel and what they
mean to us all the time. Right?" She turned quickly in the
sand and gazed into Derek's eyes.

Derek's face was shadowed. His hair was wild and
curly with the beach winds. After a pause, he said, "To be
honest, I haven't been able to stop thinking about your
great-aunt Jessabelle's diary entries. It's made me consider
how poisonous secrecy can be. That it can create cracks in
families that extend for generations."

Samantha nodded, blinking back tears.

"I didn't tell my brothers anything about your grandfather's affair or about his second family," Derek assured her. "But I did tell Patrick how angry I've been with him for years. I explained why I wasn't around for a while, that I didn't want to see him during our twenties and thirties. I told him all the things I blamed him for and that I sometimes think our family is too damaged to keep going. But more than that, I told him how much I love him. That I want to help him fight for our future. And that I know it isn't all his fault, that Brent, our father, and I carry so much of the blame."

Samantha squeezed Derek's hand, then dropped it, as it felt too intense. Softly, she told Derek how proud she was of his honesty. And when she was finished, she added, "I haven't known how to think about my grandpa Chuck's other family. I haven't even managed to look up any proof. Still, it makes sense. My father never told me why he ended his relationship with my grandfather. This must have been it."

"It's a pretty good explanation," Derek replied, "As a son, I would have felt very betrayed by something like that."

"But wouldn't you have been curious about the other side of your father's family?" Samantha asked. "I mean, I have two aunts I've never met before. Maybe they're even still over there on Martha's Vineyard. Who knows?" She pointed vaguely in the direction of Martha's Vineyard, which she'd now begun to think of as another dimension. *What had happened over there? How had her grandfather hidden two extra daughters from his wife and sons for years?*

"It's funny," Samantha whispered. "It wasn't so long

ago that I learned about my husband's own affair. Now, learning about my grandmother's affair and then my grandfather's affair, I feel like my failed marriage is just another story in a very long history of failed marriages. What on earth makes a marriage last? What makes it happy?"

Derek swallowed and stepped closer to her. There were no more than a few inches between their lips, and Samantha's brain turned anxiously. She felt like a teenager on a beach, praying she remembered all the tips her friend had told her about how to kiss.

"The thing I've learned from your great-aunt's diaries and from my own failed marriage is this," Derek began. "Honesty is the only way forward."

Samantha lifted her chin. "No secrets."

"True love means giving all of yourself. Even the messy parts."

And suddenly, his lips were upon hers, confirming what they'd both known was happening between them for many weeks. As her eyes closed, Samantha's heart banged against her ribcage, her knees dropped, and she swam in the ecstasy of being wanted, really wanted, for the first time in what felt like over a decade.

She'd known from the first moment she'd laid eyes on him that Derek was someone special. And here he was, proving her right.

Chapter Eighteen

It was time for yet another Coleman Solstice Party. To honor it, Nantucket Island temperatures had leaped to the eighties, blotching out all memory of frigid winter storms.

The event was held on a Wednesday. Samantha cleared her schedule for the second half of the day to ensure she could make it back to the Jessabelle House to set everything up. As she worked, panic struck her at odd times, and she had to frequently stand from her desk and pace the office. Once, Sharon caught her in the midst of this, scurried away, then immediately returned with a big bottle of water and a banana. "You have to keep yourself peppy today. I know how enormous this is for you."

"You're still coming, right?" Samantha eyed Sharon and took a small bite from the top of her banana. Her thoughts began to orient themselves. Perhaps she just hadn't eaten enough.

"I'll be there with bells on," Sharon said. "I've never been invited to a fancy Coleman party before."

Samantha snorted. "I can assure you; this won't be as

extraordinary as the ones in the past. My grandmother, great-aunt, and great-grandmother used to work tirelessly to make the perfect hors d'oeuvres. My great-grandfather, grandfather, and father used to find the perfect fireworks for the event and bragged that their firework display was always better than the official one put on by the city council." Samantha stitched her eyebrows together as another pang of fear came over her. "Oh gosh. I should have bought fireworks."

Sharon laughed gently. "You have food, right?"

"Too much of it."

"And drinks?"

"Too much of those too," Samantha affirmed.

"Then I think your guests will be happy, with or without the fireworks," Sharon said. "It's just like you told me this morning. You have to give your family a chance to make up for your nasty past. You said—"

"Yeah. I know. I said that I want to be open to reconciliation," Samantha repeated with a sigh. "But right now, I just want to curl up in bed and hide."

When Samantha returned to the Jessabelle House early that afternoon, she found that Rachelle had transformed her kitchen into a quasi-professional space, complete with gadgets she'd borrowed from work. At the counter and table next to it, Derek, Patrick, Brent, and Darcy slaved over canapés, tarts, homemade spring rolls, various types of fancy dips, something very small and ornate that seemed inedible but was possibly extraordinary, and three types of desserts, none of which Samantha recognized.

Behind her working chefs, Rachelle beamed. "Hi, Mom!"

"Wow." Samantha set down another load of wine and

beer, which she'd picked up on her way home. "I had no idea you were so tough."

"She's been working us like dogs for over an hour," Derek said with a funny smile.

"I told you. If you want to do this right, it's going to take time." Rachelle shrugged and turned on a heel to check on something in the oven. Darcy grimaced and continued to knead a mound of dough.

Samantha escaped Rachelle's wrath and hurried to the veranda to set up the long table upon which they planned to keep the drinks and hors d'oeuvres. Footsteps behind her told her Derek had gotten away from Rachelle, as well. Overwhelmed, Samantha turned and hurried into his arms, burrowing her head against his chest.

"I've been freaking out all day," Samantha said.

"I can see that." Derek smiled.

"I just can't decide if I should approach my father about Grandpa Chuck's affair. Or if I should just keep the peace?"

"Yeah. I keep wondering about that. Why didn't your father or uncle ever tell anyone? What kept them quiet? I mean, they hated their father so much for what he did. That amount of hate doesn't exactly breed respect for someone's secrets," Derek explained.

Samantha laced her fingers through Derek's, considering this. It did add a wedge of confusion to an already-intricate web of secrets. But before she could think of anything to say, there was a knock on the veranda steps. She turned, her heart in her throat, and discovered two familiar faces on the staircase.

It was her mother and her sister, Hilary.

"Oh goodness." Samantha hurried to the steps to

welcome them up. "You're early!" Without waiting to think twice about it, she hugged Hilary first, followed by her mother. The hug seemed to surprise Hilary, who blinked at Samantha confusedly.

"We know," Estelle explained. "But tradition says the Coleman women help out wherever needed before the solstice party."

"Ava says she's on her way," Hilary said quietly.

"I believe Shawna is too," Estelle affirmed.

Samantha grinned. "I think Great-Aunt Jessabelle and Grandma Margaret would have been pleased to see my daughters right now. They've taken to the traditions of the Coleman Solstice Party and have spent the morning and afternoon slaving away on hors d'oeuvres."

Estelle turned to inspect Derek, who stood nearly a full head above her. Unlike on a normal day of construction work, he'd donned a pair of slacks and a button-down short-sleeved shirt with a collar. Samantha thought she saw gel in his hair. *Was he nervous about meeting her parents?*

"I'm Estelle Coleman." Estelle reached out to shake Derek's hand.

To this, Derek replied, "It's wonderful to meet you. I'm Derek."

"Are you one of the brothers Samantha hired to repair the house?" Estelle asked.

"Yes, and the pleasure has been all mine," Derek confirmed.

Estelle scanned the exterior of the Jessabelle House with eyes that remembered precisely the way it had been in the seventies and eighties. "You've brought the spirit back to the old place," she said.

Samantha's heart lifted.

"I hope you're staying for our party?" Estelle asked Derek. Could she sense there was something between Sam and Derek? Was it mother's intuition?

"Sam has been gracious enough to invite my brothers and I," Derek said. "But she's asked that we not eat her out of house and home."

Estelle and Hilary chuckled good-naturedly. Hilary's eyes reflected how handsome and charming Derek was. Samantha felt herself beam with pride.

Over the next few hours, Estelle and Hilary flew into preparations for the 2023 solstice party. As Samantha fled from one disaster to another, Estelle swept the veranda of random debris, and Hilary trimmed several of the bushes around the side of the house that was visible to the party guests. Afterward, Estelle convinced her to trim the ones that weren't visible to the guests, as well. "I always feel better when I've cleaned and organized everything, even what the guests can't see," Estelle affirmed. "It makes me that much more confident as a hostess."

At this, Hilary and Samantha locked eyes. Samantha had to stop herself from bursting with laughter, and Hilary seemed the same. Later, when they accidentally met in the downstairs hallway, Hilary grabbed Samantha's arm and said, "I had no idea Mom was so crazy about tiny details."

"I'm glad I didn't inherit that," Samantha said with a laugh.

"Me too." Hilary's eyes widened. After a strange pause, she asked, "Are you nervous?"

"So nervous," Samantha whispered. "I never imagined..."

What? What did she want to tell her sister? That she'd never imagined her sister and brother would ever want to spend time with her on purpose. That she'd never imagined she'd want to repair her relationship with her father.

But before Samantha could say what she needed to say, the front door opened and closed, and her father's familiar gait echoed through the house. Roland Coleman had entered the building. It was time.

Samantha turned to watch him approach. Like always at these summer parties, he wore light pants and a linen shirt, and a pair of sunglasses that had probably cost much more than her dress. Although he did not smile, there was curiosity and eagerness etched on his face. He reached up to whip his sunglasses off, and then, like Tom Cruise in a ridiculous movie, he said, "This place looks fantastic, Sam. Aunt Jessabelle couldn't have done any better."

It took everything Samantha had not to burst into tears. "Thank you," she said. "I couldn't have done it without the Elrod Brothers." She pointed a thumb toward the kitchen, where only Brent remained hard at work over the counter. Patrick had gotten a terrible headache during food prep and retreated to his bedroom.

Suddenly, Derek appeared on the staircase, having come from upstairs. He locked eyes with Roland, who peered at him curiously. Samantha was reminded of when she'd first brought Daniel to meet her father. At the time, Roland had detested her choice of career and had extended his anger toward Daniel. Daniel hadn't managed to forgive Samantha for that.

"Dad? This is Derek," Samantha said. "And Derek, this is my father, Roland Coleman."

Derek wore that easy and handsome smile as he stepped forward. His muscles from construction work and his fishing business pulsed beneath his shirt. No, he wasn't rich and powerful, like her father— but he was kind, honest, and sincere. To Sam, that meant everything.

Derek and Roland shook hands. After that, a miracle occurred. Roland stretched his arm through the space beside him and said, "I want to know everything you did to restore this old place. Walk me through the rooms and around the grounds. I'm fascinated."

Samantha's eyes nearly fell from her head. *Was her father really taking a vested interest in a man she was falling for?*

Estelle bustled from the kitchen with a smear of flour on her cheek. As Derek and Roland disappeared outside, she whispered, "I saw Patrick go into one of the bedrooms."

Samantha nodded. Under her breath, she explained, "The brothers are going through a difficult time right now."

"But you're seeing the handsome one," Estelle probed.

Samantha's cheeks burned. "You could tell."

"Darling, anyone could tell. Even your father picked up on it." She squeezed Samantha's arm gently and said, "Now that we're old and gray, we just want everyone to be happy. It's really the only thing at the end of the day, isn't it?"

As Estelle hurried away to finish something, Samantha wondered for the millionth time if she knew about Grandpa Chuck's affair. *That wasn't the kind of thing Roland would keep from her, was it?* Then again, she could imagine him trying to preserve the Coleman reputation at all costs, even if it meant lies of omission to his wife.

By five thirty, many of the guests had begun to mill

across the veranda. They were dressed in their summertime finest: linen suits, summer dresses, and white buttondowns. Legs flashed beneath skirts, and laughter reverberated across the bluffs and off toward the dunes. As Samantha walked through the crowd, she shook hands and kissed cheeks and imagined herself to be just like Jessabelle had been all those years ago when she'd decided to take on the solstice parties for herself.

Sharon arrived around six with a man from a dating app on her arm. She hugged Samantha hard and said, "Look at this party! Look at this house! You're on top of the world!"

This meant something special coming from Sharon, as Sharon had witnessed Samantha in the depths of despair. Samantha hadn't imagined she'd ever crawl her way to the top again.

"And where is that guy you were telling me about?" Sharon demanded.

Samantha discretely pointed across the party, where Derek spoke to her uncle Grant. Samantha wondered if Derek remembered Grant from the diaries. As they spoke, Roland approached from the side and joined their conversation. At this, Derek caught Samantha's eye and smiled knowingly.

Yes. He was thinking about the scene in the diary, all right. He remembered that Roland and Grant were supposedly the only two keepers of a heinous family secret. But now, he spoke to them about something simple, like the weather or construction or the delicious hors d'oeuvres, as though nothing was wrong.

"Hey, Sis." Charlie appeared beside her, wearing a funny smile. Before Samantha knew how to react, he hugged her and said, "This reminds me of Aunt Jessabelle's old parties. I wish I was still a boy so I could get away with running around and playing ball."

Samantha laughed and pointed to the young children in the grass near the veranda. "Nobody's stopping you from joining them."

"Naw. I sold doors and windows to almost everyone here. I have to mingle for a while until I can let myself loose." He winked, then bent his head to add, "By the way, don't worry about the fireworks. I got them taken care of."

Samantha's jaw dropped. "You didn't!"

"Oh, but I did." Charlie's smile waned for a moment. He looked on the verge of saying something meaningful, something to make up for all the years of silence and tension between them. Instead, he punched her on the shoulder and said, "I better check out your daughter's cooking. I heard she went to chef school. Man, Samantha. Aren't our children incredible?"

With that, Charlie sauntered off toward the snack table, leaving Samantha with a warmth in her stomach and chest that she prayed would never leave. As she gazed across the party, watching the children play, young women gossip and giggle together, and lovers holding hands while they nibbled on hors d'oeuvres, she felt a part of the great tapestry of her very messy and complicated but loving family.

Soon, she would find a way to ask her father about Grandpa Chuck. Soon, she would get to the bottom of it. But right then, she planned to enjoy the ride.

Chapter Nineteen

Night had fallen over the solstice party. It was after eleven, and the Jessabelle House continued to vibrate with expectation. Only the children had been taken home or placed to nap in the guest bedroom, where they curled up gently next to one another and waited for their parents to take them home. Samantha remembered when her own mother had done the same for her, tucked her into a dark room to doze as the rest of her family carried on.

Incredibly, Rachelle's hors d'oeuvres, elaborate snacks, and sinful desserts hadn't run out yet. Rachelle ran the kitchen like a tight ship, ensuring that the table was well-stocked at every turn. It was when Samantha was in that kitchen, helping Rachelle to smear a raspberry glaze over a dessert, that they heard the first of the fireworks. On the veranda, the Coleman family and all their guests "oohed" and "aahed."

"You're kidding," Rachelle gasped as she raced to the window to peer out.

Samantha hurried up beside her. Sure enough, she

could make out the dark shadows of Charlie and someone else, a male, down by the beach. A moment later, they staggered back from the sight of the firework as another several orange, pink, and purple blasts took over the sky.

"Your uncle Charlie wanted to take the party to the next level," Samantha joked.

Rachelle lifted one of her eyebrows but remained quiet.

"What?" Samantha asked.

"It's just strange. Tonight, I had the longest conversations with Uncle Charlie and Aunt Hilary that I've ever had. They seemed curious about me and asked me questions about school and my future as a chef. I think they did the same to Darcy."

Samantha's heart lifted.

"I just can't understand why they decided to change so quickly," Rachelle added.

Samantha pondered this. A very deep and frightened part of her mind screamed that something terrible was about to happen, that her family was about to pull the rug out from under her. It wouldn't have been the first time. But instead of verbalizing this, she placed her hand on Rachelle's shoulder and said, "There's no reason they shouldn't absolutely adore you. You were never their messy sister. You never made Roland so angry that he cut you from the family."

Rachelle grimaced. "I don't know how to trust them."

"It's a learning process," Samantha said as the fireworks continued to blast outside. "We're all growing and changing all the time. I suppose we have to allow them to grow and change too."

Suddenly, there were footsteps on the staircase.

Samantha turned to find Derek beaming out at her from the shadows. "This has been quite a party."

Samantha laughed and squeezed Derek's hand. "I hope Patrick doesn't mind the noise."

"He'll be fine. I'm sure your brother will run out of fireworks eventually," Derek said.

"Come on. Let's go out," Samantha urged them.

Derek and Rachelle followed Samantha up and out onto the veranda, where they gathered with family members and friends and lifted their eyes to the sky. Derek remained close to her with his hand warm on her lower back. Directly beside Samantha was her cousin, Sophie, whom Samantha hadn't had the chance to speak to that evening. Just as she had on the night of the Coleman family dinner, Sophie swayed strangely, and her eyes looked glassed over and far away. Again, Samantha wondered if there was something going on.

Between blasts of the fireworks, Samantha touched Sophie's wrist and whispered, "What do you think of this?"

Sophie turned to show glazed, vacant eyes. "Oh! Hi, Sam." She seemed not to have heard Samantha's question. "Jared just loves fireworks. Sometimes, I think he's a ten-year-old boy stuck in a forty-six-year-old's body."

"Lucky him," Samantha tried. "I would love to feel ten again."

Sophie's laughter was strange. "Yes. Well. It's not exactly fun to be married to a man who wants to be ten." She paused, then giggled again. "I was so jealous when I heard you got divorced."

Samantha wasn't sure what to say. Around them, nobody else seemed to have heard. But before Samantha could answer Sophie or even try to ask her what was wrong, Sophie slipped through the crowd, crying out over the fireworks. Samantha's conclusion was very clear. Her cousin had taken something— probably too much of something. But this wasn't the time nor the place to handle a family member's drug problem. Sophie didn't seem to be in any danger, and if Samantha went out of her way to make a show of demanding what was going on, she wouldn't just destroy her relationship with Sophie. Her father and uncle would never forgive her.

Now, Samantha noticed her mother, who stood with Hilary, smiling gently. When she saw Samantha, she edged through the crowd to squeeze her elbow and say, "Isn't this exciting! It's just like the old days."

"I can't believe Charlie pulled through. I take it that's Dad down on the beach with him?"

Estelle frowned. Her eyes looked lost for a moment. "That isn't your father. That's your cousin Sophie's husband."

"Oh." Samantha furrowed her brow and scanned the crowd. For some reason, she wanted to see her father's face; she wanted to see his eyes glittering with the light from the fireworks and his face captivated by the show. But a quick scan revealed no sign of Roland. "Where is Dad?"

"I don't know where he's gone off to," Estelle said distractedly. "He's somewhere around here."

Samantha paused for a moment, her mind racing. Something in her stomach twisted. Wearing a false smile, she locked eyes with Derek and said, "I'll be right back."

"Want me to come with you?" Derek asked.

"No. I just have to check something."

Samantha wandered through the crowd, no longer conscious of the firework show. Like a hunter, she checked every corner, every nook and cranny. She analyzed the backs of men's heads and listened for the dark tone of her father's voice. Even minutes later, there was no sign of him.

Samantha entered the house quietly and walked through the shadows. Upstairs, the children who remained at the party miraculously slept through the fireworks. Patrick's door was closed, and nobody was in Samantha's bedroom. *Why would her father have gone in there, anyway?*

Samantha padded downstairs to check in the kitchen. The countertops were laden with Rachelle's ingredients and gadgets, but it was otherwise empty.

As she hovered in the living room, watching more of the never-ending firework extravaganza, something caught her eye. She twisted around to find a mysterious crack of light beneath the door to the study.

Suddenly, Samantha felt as though she'd been transported through time. It was as though her grandmother and great-aunt stood behind that door so many years after the party in 1982 and learned about Grandpa Chuck's second family over and over again. It was as though they existed forever in a nightmare.

Samantha walked toward the crack in the door, feeling she was in a dream. Outside it, she pressed her ear to the wood and listened as someone seemed to tear the room apart. It sounded like books were being shoved around, and drawers were being opened roughly. An angry man's voice muttered to himself.

It was Roland's voice. Samantha would have recognized the strength of his anger anywhere.

But what could Roland be looking for?

Exhaustion nearly made Samantha turn back. *How*

many years was she meant to go on fighting with this man? She couldn't take it anymore.

Then again, he had broken into her study and begun to go through her personal items. That was grounds for anger. *Wasn't it?*

Before she could overthink her way out of it, Samantha opened the door. She stood, seething in the doorway, as a wild-eyed Roland stood in front of a very messy desk. It seemed he'd opened every drawer. Books, folders, and papers had been flung across the floor. Sweat gleamed across his forehead as though his destruction of the study had been a kind of sport for him.

Roland locked eyes with her. In his brilliant mind, he struggled to search for the perfect excuse. There wasn't one.

And in the strange silence that fell between them, the answer to "why" landed easily in Samantha's lap.

Somehow, Roland knew about the diaries. And he didn't want her to get her hands on them.

"Hi, Dad," Samantha said finally. She crossed her arms over her chest. "Looking for something?"

Roland's cheeks were red with fear and anger. "I um. I just..." he stuttered.

"Because if you're looking for what I think you're looking for, you're about five weeks too late," Samantha shot back.

With the worst timing known to man, Charlie suddenly ran out of fireworks. The air around the Jessabelle House quieted just as Roland howled, "You have no idea what you're dealing with!"

Samantha wanted to laugh, but she felt too sad. *Why hadn't Roland felt he could approach her and ask her about the diaries himself? Why hadn't he wanted her to know*

*about the complications of their family's backstory? Why
was he so content to live in lies?*

"Get out of my study," Samantha said very slowly.

"Samantha. Just give them to me. They shouldn't
exist at all. She knew better than to have all that in
writing."

Samantha set her jaw. "She knew better than to write
in her own diaries about her own life?" It was prepos-
terous to her.

"It was bigger than her," Roland blared. "She never
married. She never knew what it was like. More than that,
she was never a Coleman."

"Oh my goodness. Of all the ridiculous things I've
heard in my life, this takes the cake." Samantha's voice
reverberated through the big house.

Suddenly, Samantha turned on her heel, then
stormed out of the room onto the veranda. When she
reached it, the guests did their best to pretend they hadn't
heard her and Roland's argument. Jared and Charlie
arrived at the veranda, their eyes confused. Someone
whispered in Jared's ear, probably explaining that
Samantha and Roland were fighting again. In the middle
of the crowd, Sophie continued to sway and peer up at
the sky as though she expected more fireworks.

Samantha steadied herself on a railing, then turned
back as Roland burst through the door. His smile was his
fake Coleman smile. Everything about this man was
surface level.

*Why had she wanted to repair her relationship with
him? Why had she trusted him at all?* Gosh, she needed
these people to leave her house. She needed peace and
quiet.

But before Samantha could begin to usher everyone

out the door, another man appeared in the doorway between the house and the veranda. It was Patrick. He looked docile and sweet, despite his six-foot frame, and as he stepped out under the moonlight, his face was illuminated.

Samantha stepped forward, ready to prepare him another plate of food or get him a glass of water. At least Patrick was good; at least he wasn't wrapped up in this Coleman nonsense.

Before that, however, Samantha's cousin Sophie cried out. Samantha turned at the sound to find Sophie stricken, her face pale. Her eyes were directed toward Patrick, who peered back at her, genuinely surprised.

There was recognition in his eyes. It was clear he'd seen her before.

"Sophie?" Samantha pushed through the crowd to try to get to her. Sophie had begun to teeter even more and seemed on the verge of falling to the ground. The woman beside her placed a hand on Sophie's shoulder to stabilize her, but it was no use.

But suddenly, Jared's voice rang through the crowd. "What in the hell is he doing here?" He then burst through the party, raised his fist, and punched Patrick directly in the nose. The crowd roared with panic. Patrick flew back and nearly hit his head on the side of the house. Jared remained above him, his hand still in a fist as he glared down at him. Derek and Brent hurried forward to create a shield between Patrick and Jared.

It all happened so quickly. As everyone rubbernecked to see what was happening, Samantha turned to those around her and suggested the party was over. Very slowly, guests began to gather their things, keeping one eye on the Patrick and Jared situation at all times.

"Jared?" Samantha was unafraid of this volatile man. "Why don't you head out for the night."

Jared's eyes were like those of a wild animal. "You're going to ask me to leave? But you're going to let that loser stay?"

On the ground, Patrick pressed a handkerchief over his bleeding nose and spoke quietly to Derek. Samantha's head spun like a washing machine.

"He's my guest," Samantha tried.

Jared scowled. "No wonder your father disowned you. You're an imbecile." He then turned on his heel and spoke to Sophie. "Let's go." He grabbed her arm, but Sophie, in a surprise burst of strength, yanked it away from him. "Let's go, Sophie," he repeated.

But there was no way Sophie was going. Instead, she hurried toward Patrick, dropped to her knees beside him, and began to whisper to him as though she'd known him all her life. Patrick lifted his head to listen. He locked eyes with her and nodded serenely. Love was reflected in their eyes.

Samantha's entire body shook with recognition.

The Colemans were full of so many secrets— and this was yet another affair. But this affair seemed tied up with the complexities of addiction, which made it far more difficult to comprehend.

"Let's go, Sophie!" Jared cried.

Samantha stepped toward him, crossed her arms, and said, "I have to ask you to leave my property, Jared."

Jared glowered at her. A moment passed. Most of the guests had rushed from the veranda, and their engines had begun to roar all the way down the long driveway. Suddenly, Sophie stood from Patrick sadly and gestured toward Jared. Samantha watched in disbelief.

"Sophie." Samantha chased after her. "You don't have to go with him."

Sophie looked at Samantha as though she'd lost her mind.

"You know, you can come talk to me about this," Samantha said, watching as Jared led Sophie toward the veranda steps. "My office is downtown, and my door is always open."

Jared yanked around to blare a final, "Mind your own business, you creep." After that, they disappeared into the darkness, tracing the route back to their car. Very soon came the sounds of their engine and the squeal of their tires. They were gone.

Chapter Twenty

1984

Jessabelle Oliver had always been two years younger than her older sister, Margaret. This meant that throughout childhood, Jessabelle had been like Margaret's shadow. Whatever Margaret had done or eaten or said, Jessabelle had wanted it too. Once, as teenagers, this had gone to an extreme when Jessabelle had briefly dated a man Margaret had dumped. In their twenties, they'd been able to laugh about it, but at the time, Margaret's rage had made Jessabelle miserable. All she'd wanted in the world was for her sister to love and respect her. All she'd wanted was to be as close as two people could be.

Now, Jessabelle was forty-nine years old. Despite her age, it was the eighties now, which meant women were afforded new social rules. She could date all kinds of men — sailors, tradesmen, technicians, chefs, and men who waited for their fathers to die so they would get their inheritance. It was true that Jessabelle still dreamt of Arnold, that he was the only man she'd ever truly loved. But it was also true that Jessabelle probably had more fun than most other women her age. She didn't have to pack anyone's lunch. She didn't have to force anyone to do homework. And she certainly didn't have to answer to anyone when she did what she pleased.

On top of that, she'd begun a small friendship with her great-niece, Samantha, who seemed slightly different from the others in her family. Her eyes were big and curious, and she asked Jessabelle questions that seemed more advanced than her age should have allowed. Frequently, Estelle dropped Samantha off at the Jessabelle House, where Jessabelle taught her card games and baked her cookies. It was her one shot at being a "grandmother," and it pleased her more than she'd expected.

"She seems like a sweet girl," Margaret, who was fifty-one now, said of Samantha. They were seated on their favorite beach as the waves swelled toward them. A half-eaten picnic sat on the blanket between them and would surely be attacked by ants soon. "She doesn't look at me very much."

"She's young and shy," Jessabelle said.

Margaret tied her gray-streaked hair into a ponytail. Despite their age, neither of them had given up on their long hair. "I can't help but feel distanced from all of my grandchildren," she admitted. "I feel so unwanted."

Jessabelle nodded. It was rare that Margaret wanted to discuss what they'd learned on that fateful day at the solstice party two years ago. Since then, she'd watched Margaret diminish to nothing. She'd lost perhaps twenty pounds, and she hardly spoke to anyone except Jessabelle. Her heart had been completely broken.

"Have you considered..." Jessabelle began.

But Margaret shook her head. "I told you. I can't get divorced."

"But wouldn't you be happier living outside of this lie?" Jessabelle demanded. "I mean, when Chuck comes home from his travels, don't you hate that he pretends he doesn't have this whole other life?"

"Of course I do!" Margaret shot back. "But another part of me still loves him. I've given my entire life to him. What would I do if I asked for a divorce? Would I get an apartment? Die alone in a room somewhere?"

Jessabelle was quiet, and Margaret hurried to correct herself. "I'm sorry. It's not that I think being alone is so bad," she said, although this was clearly what she thought.

"It's fine. Being alone took some getting used to," Jessabelle said. "I do think you could get used to it, though. You could meet someone else, someone who respected you enough not to lie to you."

Margaret grimaced. She removed a grape from its stem and sliced it in half with her teeth, then said, "The worst is that neither of my sons has come forward with the truth. Neither of them respects me enough to take me aside and tell me the truth."

Jessabelle had no idea what to say to that. She'd been curious about that, as well— and had frequently been overwhelmed with anger by it. She wanted to take Roland to the side and berate him. Then again, Roland seemed sharper and more difficult than ever, as though he whittled himself into his father's form.

"Roland and Grant hardly speak to Chuck anymore,

though," Margaret continued. "They hardly come over if they know he's home."

"They're angry," Jessabelle breathed.

"Maybe they're not angry enough," Margaret said.

That night, Chuck was away "on business." Jessabelle went to their place, showered, and began to prepare dinner for herself and Margaret. Margaret sat glumly at the kitchen island with her chin on her fist. She'd dragged the television in from the living room, and it played a crime show.

"Chuck doesn't like it when I have the TV in here," Margaret said.

Jessabelle hated that she agreed with Chuck. The noise of the television was irritating. It seemed proof that Margaret couldn't be alone with her thoughts.

Jessabelle made steak, mashed potatoes, and corn. Together, they sat at the dining room table, which was normally suited for ten people, as Margaret moved her food around her plate. Jessabelle wanted to demand Margaret take "at least five bites," but she knew she couldn't speak to her like that.

"What do you think he'd do? If I confronted him about his second family?" Margaret asked suddenly. She'd never said this before.

Jessabelle considered this. "Why don't you? I'd love to hear what he'd say."

"Then again, he'd probably just leave me immediately." Margaret ate a very small spoonful of corn.

"You don't know what he'd do," Jessabelle pointed out.

Margaret swallowed her corn and remained silent for a moment. Then, she asked, "What do you think my life would have been like if I'd left Chuck for Dr. Rushford?"

Jessabelle wanted to tell her sister that her life probably would have been very similar. That Trevor Rushford hadn't seemed respectful of her wants or needs, either. But perhaps all Margaret had these days were her daydreams, and Jessabelle didn't want to kill them.

"You probably would have had to have more children," Jessabelle said.

"Oh..." Margaret looked wistful. "They would have been darling children, right? And I could have been a doctor's wife! Gosh. I really should have married him when I had the chance. All the other nurses were so jealous that he gave me so much attention. I felt like the queen of that hospital."

At that moment, Margaret looked so tremendously sad that Jessabelle's heart nearly broke in two.

* * *

The phone in Jessabelle's kitchen blared at two in the morning. Jessabelle made her way toward it, bleary-eyed, and answered it on the fourth ring. It was Chuck.

On the other line, Chuck blubbered incoherently. Jessabelle wanted to scream at him to start making sense. But slowly, she began to piece together what had happened. He'd returned home after midnight "from a business trip" to find Margaret "passed out" on the sofa. When he'd tried to wake her up, she hadn't moved. He'd called the ambulance, who had pronounced her dead at the scene.

Dead.

Jessabelle's sister was dead at fifty-one.

Jessabelle was too shocked to feel anything else. Her jaw hung open as Chuck wailed into the phone. Images from their final night together played through her mind—of Margaret hardly eating her corn, of Jessabelle putting her steak in the fridge "for later," and of Margaret saying again and again that she should have left Chuck for Trevor if only to avoid the pain of what Chuck had done.

For two years, Margaret had lived in agony, knowing that Chuck had built a life with someone else. And now, she'd found a way to run away from that pain.

Eventually, Jessabelle hung up on Chuck. She hated him.

The funeral for Jessabelle's very favorite person in the world was held on a Thursday in August. The man Jessabelle was dating offered to go with her, but Jessabelle refused. She already planned to break up with him within the month. He would be deadweight.

Jessabelle wore one of Margaret's black dresses as a way to feel closer to her. When she arrived at the funeral home a half hour before the ceremony was set to begin, Chuck was in conversation with the funeral director, and his face was stricken. Jessabelle wanted to tell Chuck to leave. He had no right to be there. He had been the cause of her broken heart, as far as she was concerned.

Margaret lay in her coffin, looking serene, beautiful, and very unlike herself. Because she'd lost so much weight in the past two years, the funeral director had only been able to do so much about her sunken cheeks. Her hair was spread over the coffin pillow like a princess, and she wore a light pink dress, one of her favorites. Jessabelle had insisted on it.

At the funeral, both Roland and Grant spoke. They told a story about a woman who'd given her "all" to their family, that she was selfless, lovely, and the best mother they could have had. "She died too young," Roland said.

"I expected so many more years together. I expected her to watch my children grow up alongside me. She deserved that, after all the work she did to raise Grant and I." After another pause, he seemed to glare at his father before he added, "Although she was born an Oliver, Mom was every bit a Coleman. She exuded the pride, intellect, and goodwill of all Colemans. And I hope, going forward in my life, I embody everything she stood for and make her proud."

The wake was held at Chuck and Margaret's house. Jessabelle felt very quiet yet volatile, as though she was a bomb about to go off. In the dining room, she ate a bowl of clam chowder and spoke to Roland's wife, Estelle, but could hardly remember what they'd spoken about after. It was only when Estelle spoke of Chuck and Margaret that Jessabelle gleaned Estelle didn't know about the affair and second family. Roland and Grant had kept it fully under wraps.

Jessabelle continued to refill her wineglass. The alcohol made the world a little fuzzier and easier to handle. From across rooms of the house, she glared at Chuck, who stood around, being consoled by friends and acquaintances. None of them knew what he'd done.

Perhaps because of the three glasses of wine, Jessabelle found herself hunting for Roland and Grant. She decided she couldn't leave the wake without giving them a piece of her mind. After all, she'd been there for their births, watching as Margaret had destroyed herself to bring them into the world. *Why hadn't they respected her enough to uphold her needs? Why had they done this?*

Jessabelle eventually cornered them in the kitchen. Through slurred words, she said, "I can't believe either of you."

Grant and Roland exchanged confused glances.

"Aunt Jessabelle, we're both just so sad," Roland said. "We haven't known how to handle this."

"Yeah. There's no how-to manual," Grant affirmed.

But Jessabelle wouldn't let them get away with this. "Why did you keep it to yourself? Why did you let her suffer like that?"

Grant and Roland frowned.

"Come on. We all know what I'm talking about," Jessabelle rasped. "She knew all about his second family. She knew you knew. And for years, she wasted away, destroying herself, because she realized she wasn't worthy of the truth."

Roland's jaw dropped. Grant looked on the verge of a nervous breakdown.

But before they could speak, Chuck stepped into the kitchen to get something. He stopped short in the kitchen, eyeing them fearfully.

"All good in here?" he asked.

"Just fine," Roland said icily.

Chuck nodded and backed out of the kitchen. He looked like he wanted to say something but kept it to himself.

And suddenly, it occurred to Jessabelle what must have happened.

"Oh my God. He paid you off." She took a step back and pointed at them. "Of course. Why didn't I figure it out before?" Tears started to roll down her face.

The look on Roland's face told her it was the truth. Both Grant and Roland were panicked. Roland was about to say something, but nothing came out.

"Don't! Don't you dare say a word," Jessabelle shot out. "Chuck Coleman is made of money, and he produced two sons who uphold money above all things, including their mother. You should be ashamed of yourselves."

Jessabelle grabbed a bottle of wine from the counter, stormed through the crowded rooms, and stepped into the August heat. As she walked home, tears streamed down her cheeks, and the wine bottle banged against her thigh. All she wanted in the world just now was to call her sister to ask her to meet her at the beach for a picnic. *"Isn't it a perfect day for a swim?"*

But she never would call her sister again. Margaret was gone, leaving Jessabelle alone for good.

Chapter Twenty-One

Present Day

"Well. Nobody can say I didn't try to throw a good party." Samantha sat on the veranda the morning after the solstice party with a mug of coffee and stared glumly out at the Atlantic horizon. She hadn't drunk enough wine for a hangover, but her head and heart felt very heavy, and she wanted to curl up in bed and abandon the world.

Derek, Rachelle, and Darcy sat at the table with her, nursing mugs of coffee in quiet reflection. Nobody knew what to say about the events of the party. After Sophie and Jared had left, Patrick had retreated to his room, asking to be left alone. Of this, Samantha had asked Derek if he knew anything about Patrick's love life, and Derek said he knew nothing.

After they finished their coffee, Rachelle and Darcy packed up their things, kissed their mother goodbye, and fled back downtown for their work shifts. This left Samantha and Derek alone in the splendor of the sun, surrounded still by the leftover debris from the party. It would take them hours to clean.

"I just can't believe Patrick would sleep with a married woman," Derek muttered, clearly distracted. "He knows my wife cheated on me. He knows how sensitive that issue is."

"Maybe he didn't know she was married."

Derek shrugged.

"Well, based on the way Sophie's husband was acting last night, I have a hunch their relationship isn't the coziest," Samantha said.

"Understatement of the century," Derek agreed. "Do you think that's why she started using?"

Samantha closed her eyes, exhausted. "It's difficult to know why anyone starts using. Maybe Sophie has used for a long time and managed to keep it under control until now. Maybe she's lived a double life."

Derek's eyes glittered in recognition. Samantha knew he thought about her grandpa Chuck even before he said so. "So, you really think your dad was looking for the diaries?"

"He admitted he was," Samantha said. "It was like he wanted to destroy the evidence."

"But he didn't find them?"

"No! I put them back in the wall behind the bookshelf," Samantha said. "There were too many people milling around. I didn't want them to get into the wrong hands."

Derek nodded and thought for a moment. Samantha began to collect the wineglasses and beer bottles in her immediate vicinity, promising herself she would never host another family party again.

"When did your grandfather pass away?" Derek asked.

Samantha lifted a half-drunk beer bottle from the veranda ground and blinked over at him. "Oh!" She shook her head aggressively as the realization took hold. "I don't know if he actually did."

Derek laughed with surprise. "You don't know if your own grandfather is alive?"

"I told you. My father has hardly talked to him since, well, since he learned about the family on Martha's Vineyard," Samantha said hurriedly. She abandoned the half-drunk bottle of beer and returned to the table. "If there had been a funeral, I guess we wouldn't have gone."

"Your dad and uncle know if he's still alive, I bet," Derek said. "It's important to know where the enemy is at all times."

Samantha bobbed her head. "I can't ask them, though. We have to figure this out ourselves." She then regarded the mess around them, which glittered beneath the summer light. "The cleaning can wait. Want to head into town with me? I know the woman who works in the public records office. Maybe she has some information."

* * *

Derek drove them downtown in his construction company truck. After they parked, they grabbed second cups of coffee from a kiosk, where they flirted in line, both simmering with expectation for what they might discover. As they walked toward the records office, Samantha thanked Derek for his help, and Derek just laughed and said, "I feel like I'm on a treasure hunt or something."

The woman at the records office greeted Samantha happily and directed them to the back room, where they could scour through birth certificates, death certificates, tax records, and changes of address. It was an old-fashioned thing to change your address with the government, Samantha knew, but Chuck would have been ninety-one by now. It was the type of thing he would have done.

Given what Samantha knew from the diaries, what she discovered wasn't surprising. Chuck had updated his forwarding address in the year 1985, one year after Margaret's death. At this time, he reported himself as a new resident of Oak Bluffs on Martha's Vineyard.

"He must have gone to live with his other family full-time," Derek breathed.

Samantha nodded excitedly. "There's a phone number. Should we call it?"

Samantha took a photo of the number and address and returned the file to its dusty box. At the front desk, she waved goodbye to the woman who worked there, then led Derek onto the street. Once there, she dialed the number of Chuck Coleman's 1985 address and waited as the call blared across the Nantucket Sound.

An older woman answered the phone. "Hello?"

"Hi." How could she proceed? "My name is Samantha, and I'm looking for Chuck Coleman."

"Oh goodness. Yes. I used to get calls for him all the time," the older woman said. "I think he changed phone numbers."

Samantha could hardly speak. "Do you know how I could get a hold of him?"

"I believe he moved to that retirement facility outside

of Oak Bluffs," the older woman said. "I'm a friend of a friend of Oriana's, and that's what she told me."

Oriana. Samantha remembered that name from the diary. *Was she one of Chuck's daughters?*

Samantha thanked the woman for her help, then got off the phone and explained what she'd learned to Derek. Derek had heard of this retirement facility and immediately called them to ask about a specific resident. He explained he was a long-lost relative of Chuck's and that he's been anxious to restore contact. The facility told Derek that Chuck had been a resident there for over five years. When Derek asked if he was taking visitors these days, the staff member explained that today's visiting hours began at two and ended at six. They could still make it.

* * *

Samantha had never been out on Derek's fishing boat. As he turned on the engine with practiced ease, she watched the tourists on shore as they milled along the boardwalk, watching the boats and taking photographs of the water. Although Derek had said he hadn't found time to take many clients out fishing that summer, several fishing poles were still stored along the walls of the boat, latched into place. Their hooks sparkled in the sun.

The boat ride from Nantucket to Martha's Vineyard gave Samantha time to think. With Derek in the captain's seat and his hand on the wheel, she placed her head on his shoulder and closed her eyes against the breeze.

How many times had Chuck Coleman done this route from Nantucket to Martha's Vineyard to see his other family? Had he ever considered his "other" family to be his "better" family?

"Do you think Chuck had this other family as a way to get back at Margaret for her affair?" Derek asked now as the island of Martha's Vineyard crept up from the western horizon.

"It's not nice, but it's possible," Samantha said.

"Nothing about this is nice," Derek affirmed. "I just can't understand why he wouldn't have asked for a divorce rather than lead two lives."

"He's a Coleman," Samantha answered simply. "Image is everything. It's why my dad didn't want me to have the diaries. He's worried I'll taint his reputation. And maybe it's true that I want to. I want to take King Coleman down from his ivory tower and remind him he's human too."

Derek tied up the fishing boat in Oak Bluffs harbor, and Samantha stepped out onto the dock, which shook beneath her as she walked. Derek hurried up behind her and laced his fingers through hers. They were a team.

Because the retirement facility was on the outskirts of Oak Bluffs, they hailed a taxi to take them the rest of the way. Throughout the trip, the driver mistook them for tourists and spoke to them excitedly about their trip.

"Have you ever been to Martha's Vineyard before?" he asked.

"Never," Derek said. "My wife and I just got married, and we thought it was the perfect place for a honeymoon."

At this, the driver burst into surprised laughter. "Congratulations! My gosh!" He glanced in the rear-view mirror. "You two lovebirds are going to have the time of your life."

When they reached the retirement facility, paid up, and left a big tip for the driver, Samantha giggled and wrapped her arms around Derek. "Why did you lie to the driver?"

"I don't know. Isn't it fun to pretend to be someone else for a minute?" Derek asked. "Besides, it was a test. If you freaked out at the idea of spending some real time with me, I would know you weren't really into me."

Samantha paused, her heart thudding. This was the first time Derek had approached the idea of a real, solid relationship. Before this, they'd just spent every moment possible together, all while avoiding the topic of how powerful their connection was.

"I think I'm really into this," Samantha admitted.

Outside the retirement facility, her new boyfriend kissed her with his arms around her. When the kiss broke, Samantha felt woozy with her feelings for him.

Inside the retirement facility, they explained they had come to see Chuck Coleman. When she said his name, Samantha stuttered with disbelief. She hadn't seen her grandfather in the flesh since she'd been a little girl. *Would he even remember her?*

The nurse led them into the living area of the facility, where residents spent time either together, alone, or with their guests. Several played board games or cards while others drank coffee and tea by a fake fireplace. Some were watching television with headphones on to ensure the sound didn't bother anyone else. As they walked, the nurse spoke about the facility's belief in the power of community. "We make sure everyone has a friend here," she explained.

Samantha couldn't have agreed with her more. In her experience, when her clients cleaned up and became sober, they missed their addiction community so much that they frequently relapsed. So often, people neglected friendships, neighbors, and family and lived their lives alone. It wasn't right.

"There he is," the nurse said with a bright smile. She'd stopped in front of a collection of chess tables, where two old men with white hair hunched over a game. "It's hard to drag him away from a game of chess. He says it's good for his mind." In a louder voice, she said, "Mr. Coleman? You have visitors."

At the moment that it took for her grandfather to turn her head, Samantha nearly turned on her heel and fled. This was the man her father hated; this was the man her great-aunt Jessabelle blamed for Margaret's death. Yet here he was in the flesh, vibrant at ninety-one, his mind healthy enough that he could play rounds and rounds of chess.

Chuck Coleman looked at Samantha and Derek with open and honest eyes. He looked like he wanted to know them, as though he searched every name he'd ever known.

"I'm sorry to interrupt your game," Samantha said as the nurse inched away. "But we were wondering if we could talk to you for a little while."

Chuck surely heard the urgency in her voice. Softly, he asked his opponent if he could take a break, and then he wheeled his wheelchair over to the corner of the room, across from two cushioned chairs with floral patterns. Samantha and Derek sat at the edge of the chairs, and tension spilled through the space between the three of them. *How could she begin?*

"Chuck? I don't know how to say this, so I'll just come out with it. My name is Samantha, and I'm..."

But Chuck interrupted. "You're Roland's daughter!" His jaw dropped with disbelief. For a moment, Samantha thought he was going to tell her to leave him immediately. But the smile that played across his face after that could have been nothing but joyful. He reached across the space between them, took her hand, and blubbered with abrupt tears. "I'm sorry. I don't mean to act like this."

Samantha couldn't help but begin to cry too.

"I just never imagined I'd see any of you again," Chuck said softly. "It's been well over thirty years since I left Nantucket for good. I figured it was too late."

Samantha was caught off guard by the love in his eyes. Jessabelle had written about a black-hearted, evil man. But the man before Samantha now was soft, old, and filled with regret.

Tentatively, Samantha explained she'd just learned why her father had cut Chuck from his life. Chuck nodded, wincing slightly.

"I can't imagine Roland was the one to tell you," Chuck said.

"No. My father was never very fond of me," Samantha explained. "He wouldn't have been forthcoming about any family secrets."

"What could he not like about you?" Chuck looked flabbergasted.

Samantha waved, suddenly embarrassed. It was too difficult to explain.

Chuck placed his hands over his face and sighed into them. "I really regret how it all played out. I handled everything like a child. I wanted what I wanted when I wanted it. And then, when my sons found out what was going on, I panicked and bribed them not to say anything.

Isn't that heinous?" He allowed his hands to drop, and his eyes were like marbles.

Jessabelle had suspected he'd paid Roland and Grant off, but this was confirmation. Samantha wondered how much had been enough.

"Oh, but I had no idea Margaret knew," Chuck said, his eyes to the ground. "I paid out four million dollars, two to each of my sons, and still, Margaret knew. She withered away because of it. Did I care? Of course I did, but my hands were tied. My daughters were young. Mia and I had problems of our own. I couldn't hold all the stories in my head any longer. And when Margaret passed away, I thought, well— it was finally time to live in the truth."

Samantha's heart cracked at the edges. Two million dollars to each of his sons for their silence! It was so evil. Yet here he was, admitting it.

After a moment, Samantha spoke. "I know Margaret had an affair of her own. One you found out about and forced her to end."

Chuck grimaced. "Dr. Rushford."

"We've been wondering. Was her affair the reason you had one of your own?" Samantha asked.

Grandpa Chuck considered this and nodded. "I think it started off that way. I was so angry she'd betrayed me. The worst of it was I think she really loved that man, Trevor Rushford. I couldn't stand that I'd driven her into his arms. And I suppose I wanted to show off a little bit and prove that I could do the same. It just got so out of hand."

That was an understatement, Samantha thought.

As minutes passed, Samantha and Grandpa Chuck found ways to talk around the darkness of their past. Samantha showed photographs of Rachelle and Darcy and properly introduced Derek, who she called her boyfriend for the first time.

Afterward, Chuck told bits and pieces about his life on Martha's Vineyard. He'd been able to retire and focus more on his daughters, Oriana and Meghan. He'd fallen in love with the island, even though it had never felt entirely like home.

Just before visitation finished for the afternoon, Samantha heard herself ask her grandfather a burning question.

"Would you ever want your two families to meet each other?"

At this, Chuck bristled. "I don't know if I'm strong enough for that. I'm too enveloped in shame for what I did, but that would be a question for my daughters." He paused for a moment, then added, "But more than anything, I'd like to see my boys again. I want to apologize to them properly, the way I should have all those years ago. And I want to hear how their lives have gone over the past thirty-two years. I wonder if you could ask them to come to see me. I wonder if you could make that happen?"

Chapter Twenty-Two

The Sunrise Cove Bistro was a top-rated dinner destination on the island of Martha's Vineyard. When Derek asked their second taxi driver about it, the driver talked at length about Wes Sheridan, who had owned the bistro and inn for decades, along with his daughters, the Sheridan Sisters, who had picked up the reins as he'd aged. "Those sisters used to hate their father," the taxi driver gossiped as they drove toward the Bistro. "But turns out it was all a misunderstanding if you can believe it. They're thick as thieves now. If you ask me, they all spent too many years being too stubborn for their own good."

Once at the Sunrise Cove Bistro, Samantha and Derek sat at an outdoor table and watched the water quietly. Derek nursed a beer as Samantha sipped a chardonnay. Around them, Martha's Vineyard tourists and locals drank wine, ate dishes of salmon and trout, and shared cheese plates. Laughter rang through the June night.

"I couldn't believe what the driver said about the stubborn family who owns this place," Samantha said. "It almost felt like he was talking about the Colemans."

"I guess it goes to show all families have a lot of baggage," Derek said. "Mine certainly does."

They'd skipped lunch and now ordered two appetizers, two entrées, and a dessert to share. They were starving. It was the first dinner they'd shared as a couple, but it was also weighted with the heaviness of what they'd just done. After thirty-two years, a member of the Coleman family had met with Chuck Coleman. What she'd discovered was that he was rather kind and filled with regret, which had shifted her opinion of him.

She had to talk to her father about him. She had to find a way to heal the wounds of the past.

"You know, any of these people around us could be my extended family," Samantha whispered, eyeing the tables on the patio. "That woman over there could be my half aunt! And maybe her son is my half cousin!"

Derek laughed and placed his hand over hers on the tablecloth. "I take it you want to meet them."

"Yes, I'm only human. I'm curious," Samantha admitted. "I mean, their experiences with Chuck Coleman couldn't be more different than my father's and uncle's. I'm amazed at the idea that one man could be so many different people at once, you know?"

Before Derek could answer, Samantha's phone buzzed on the top of the table. The name across the screen said: **SOPHIE.**

Samantha's eyes widened. In a flash, she answered it. "Sophie?"

"Hi." Sophie's voice sounded so far away and muffled. "Samantha, I hate to bother you like this."

"I told you to call me any time," Samantha reminded her. "What's wrong?"

"I was wondering if you could meet tonight?" Sophie asked.

"Sure. I'm off the island right now, but I should be back soon. Where do you want to meet?"

Sophie was quiet for a few moments. "I'm already at your place. So, let's just meet here if that's okay."

Samantha agreed.

* * *

On the way back from Martha's Vineyard, Samantha and Derek spoke at length about the drama of Patrick and Sophie's story.

"There's so much we don't understand yet," Samantha insisted. "We have to hear them out and not jump to any conclusions."

"I just hope they're not pushing each other to use," Derek said fearfully. "That's how it works, right? So often, couples have to get sober together and stay sober together, or else."

"They're not technically a couple, I guess?" Samantha tried, although even she didn't believe it. The way Sophie had looked at Patrick had told her everything she needed to know. They were in love.

Derek and Samantha pulled up outside the Jessabelle House just after ten that night. Twilight had fallen, and stars twinkled just above the horizon line. On the veranda, two figures sat with their arms around each other, gazing out toward the water.

Samantha and Derek mounted the steps to the veranda wordlessly. By the time they reached the veranda, both Sophie and Patrick were standing expectantly. Sophie was very pale, but she seemed solid and sober. Patrick looked the same.

"Oh, Sophie." Samantha hurried forward and hugged her cousin, genuinely surprised and glad she'd made the call. She'd worried she would fall deeper into Jared's world and eventually find a way to destroy herself for good.

At the table on the veranda, Samantha poured everyone lemonade, and they sat and made very brief small talk. The nature of Sophie's visit was like an iceberg — it went deep below the surface and was potentially threatening to everyone there.

Over the table, Sophie and Patrick linked hands. Their union was strong.

Finally, Derek asked, "How long have you two been together?"

"Over a year," Sophie said firmly.

Samantha was surprised but didn't show it.

"Gosh, how do I start this story?" Sophie searched for the right words. "Sam, you know I've been married to Jared since I was twenty-one. I had never dated anyone else. Although he was cruel and manipulative, I was pretty sure that's what it meant to be married."

Samantha wrinkled her nose. She didn't say it, but she'd felt the same way about Daniel.

"I had dabbled in drug use as a teenager, but I didn't get serious about it until I was in my late thirties, which sounds ridiculous," Sophie continued. "At first, it was just prescription drugs, but Jared didn't like that. He thought people on the island would start to talk if they saw me picking up pills at the pharmacy, and he forbade me from getting more. By that point, I'd figured out I was basically addicted. I literally couldn't go a day without them. So, I did what I had to do and met the people I needed to meet."

Sophie flinched and glanced at Patrick, who continued to hold her hand tightly. "When I met Patrick, I understood I'd never been in love before. Not really. Not like this."

"Did Jared ever find out?" Derek asked.

Patrick nodded, looking sullen. "That wasn't the first time he's punched me in the nose."

"You can leave him, Sophie," Samantha said, her words urgent.

"For a long time, I didn't think I could," Sophie told her. "But then I saw you at your party. You looked happier than I'd seen you in decades, floating across the veranda with this handsome man beside you. Although I was high as a kite, I still recognized you to be Patrick's brother. The three of you look so similar."

Derek and Patrick laughed gently.

"Anyway, this morning, when Jared went for a run, I packed my bag and came here," Sophie continued. "I can't live like that anymore. But more than that, I want to get clean. I have to get clean. I want my life to feel meaningful again." Her eyes widened as she gazed into Samantha's. "Will you please help me?"

Samantha nodded, her heart extending to both of them. "I have to make a few phone calls, pull a few strings. But I think I could get you into rehab in a few days at the most. Would you be willing to go?"

"We'll go together," Patrick said. "Because we're in this together, now."

Sophie bobbed her head. "I'm ready. There's no other way."

Chapter Twenty-Three

For the second time in just a few weeks, Samantha found herself on the back porch of her parents' estate, a place she'd kept her distance from for years. With a glass of iced tea sweating in her hand, she sat next to her mother and watched the birds fly in and out of the trees, their wings flashing in the sun. On the table sat a tall stack of very old diaries, every single one of which she'd scoured for information about a woman she'd loved. For not the first time, Samantha remembered that through all the drama of the previous two months, she'd also carried the loss of Jessabelle. The diaries had helped her get through the grieving process.

Death was the only expected thing. But you had to do your best with the time you had. Perhaps Jessabelle's diaries reminded her of that most of all.

"It just breaks my heart to hear about Sophie," Estelle said now, her gaze on the trees. "Your uncle Grant is beside himself."

"He shouldn't be," Samantha assured her. "For years,

Sophie was alone in her addiction. Now, she actually has the strength to try to get better. It's hopeful, really. It means she wants to live. Unfortunately for the Colemans, that means her secret is out in the open."

Estelle's face crumpled. Very quietly, she whispered, "We've created a very dangerous world, haven't we?"

"The Coleman way has been ingrained in our family for generations," Samantha said. "But there's no reason we can't stop it in its tracks right now."

Samantha hadn't yet told her mother or father about her trip to Martha's Vineyard. Estelle had learned about Sophie through Sophie's mother, who'd cried over the phone that Sophie had left Jared and checked into rehab. Rumor had it Jared was so outraged and embarrassed that he'd left the island. Samantha hadn't said anything about Sophie and Patrick's affair; it wasn't her business who they decided to love.

Estelle spread her palm over the stack of worn diaries. "You've read all of them, then?"

Samantha nodded. "She'd hidden them in the wall. When I found them, they became a sort of obsession."

"Your great-aunt was one of the first women I knew who did exactly what she wanted when she wanted to. I always respected her for that," Estelle said. Under her breath, she added, "At some point, her opinion of Roland seemed to change. She looked at him like..." Estelle shook her head as though she wanted to say something too heavy. "Well, let's just say that I could tell she didn't really like him anymore. And sometimes, I wondered if she extended that dislike to me. After all, I was married to Roland. Perhaps she didn't respect me because of it."

Samantha remembered all the passages Jessabelle had

written about Estelle. She'd scribed her as an intelligent and creative woman, one who was "unlike the other Colemans."

"According to the diaries, she really respected you for being a writer," Samantha said. "I think she saw something of herself in you."

Estelle's eyes glittered with curiosity. It was strange, Samantha knew, to see yourself and your life reflected in someone else's memories.

Deep in the house, the front door of the estate opened and closed. Roland's voice hollered hello. Fear rolled through Samantha as Estelle popped up and asked Roland to come to the back porch. In only a moment, he stood in the doorway, peering down at his middle child and the stack of diaries. He looked very tired. Samantha felt tired too.

"Roland, Samantha says she has something to talk to us about," Estelle said tentatively. "Would you mind sitting down?"

Roland stepped around the porch table and sat across from Samantha. He carried a confident aura, and his sandalwood cologne clung to the air around him. Like Estelle, he placed his hand over the stack of diaries and said, "So many years."

Samantha nodded. With Derek, she'd practiced how she wanted to explain what she'd done, but now, her tongue stalled.

"Do you remember that day I asked you if Grandma Margaret had ever had an affair?" Samantha asked softly.

Roland's eyes lifted. "I do. It's when it occurred to me that Jessabelle's diaries were in your hands. I hadn't thought of them in years." He paused and traced his teeth with his tongue. "I realized they were the last piece of evidence against our family name."

"And you wanted to destroy them," Samantha confirmed.

"Not destroy..." Roland trailed off. He then locked eyes with her and said, "You have to understand, Samantha. This family secret has been such a heavy burden for decades. Grant and I have struggled endlessly to keep our family name from being tainted. It's practically been our lifelong mission. Suddenly, I realized that all of our struggles to keep this secret could be destroyed in the blink of an eye just because of the diaries. And I panicked."

"Is that why you wanted me to have a family party? So you could get inside the house?"

Roland sputtered sadly. "Maybe that's how it started. I don't know." He paused for a moment.

"What family secret?" Estelle whispered. "What on earth are you talking about? Margaret had an affair?"

"I didn't know about that," Roland said.

Samantha explained what she knew as simply as possible: that Grandpa Chuck had been so consumed with his second business and its success that Margaret had decided to use her nursing degree and work at the hospital. While there, she'd fallen head over heels with a man named Dr. Trevor Rushford. When Chuck had learned of the affair, he'd demanded she break things off and quit her job.

"But I think he couldn't forgive her and resented her for it," Samantha added. "And he found himself lost in an affair of his own."

"My goodness," Estelle muttered.

Roland lifted his shoulders. "So, you know everything now. Every last bit of darkness in our family's past."

"I know more than that," Samantha admitted softly.

Roland looked at her accusatorially.

Before she could chicken out, she said, "I went to Martha's Vineyard. I went to see him."

Roland's jaw dropped open. Estelle gasped into her hand.

"He's an old man, Dad," Samantha continued. "Ninety-one years old and riddled with regrets. He hates the way everything panned out. He..."

Roland's nostrils flared. "He abandoned our family and then created a second one! Do you know how many times he told me about 'the Coleman way' and about how essential it was to 'uphold our family's image'? He drilled that into me as a child, as a teenager, and as a young man. The hypocrisy is astounding, isn't it?"

Samantha's mouth felt very dry. "To me, it just seems like this imaginary 'Coleman way' just doesn't work. I mean, you didn't talk to me for years just because I wanted to go into social work, to take my own path and not follow yours."

For a moment, Roland was very quiet. She'd cornered him.

"Listen," Samantha continued quietly. "You don't have to do anything you don't want to do, but Grandpa Chuck said all he wants in the world is to see you and Grant again. Would you consider going to his retirement facility? Would you consider hearing him out?"

Roland blinked at her, at a loss for words. Estelle reached across the table and gripped his hand.

"He's so old, Dad," Samantha added. "He's not going to be around much longer. And if there's anything I learned from Jessabelle's diaries, it's that we have a very limited time on this earth. Shouldn't we find ways to forgive each other and move on?

"I'm open to forgiveness, Dad. I'm open to forgiving myself for the ways I've treated you, and I'm open to forgiving you for ostracizing me for my career decisions. In my field, we learn this is the only way forward. It's the only way to build a hopeful path to the future."

Chapter Twenty-Four

Several days later, Derek agreed to use his fishing boat to take Roland, Uncle Grant, and Samantha to Martha's Vineyard. On the boat, Roland and Grant sat side-by-side and clenched their jaws with panic. Although they were clean, well-dressed, and confident, their eyes stirred with memories they couldn't forget and fears around a man who probably would have cracked a rib if he'd yelled too loudly.

It was funny how you never lost your fears from child-hood. They clung to you and made you vulnerable forever.

Despite pushing herself, Samantha still had very little power over her fears around her father. Even now, she kept her distance from him, standing at the steering wheel with Derek and muttering under her breath.

"They hate that you know about this," she whispered. "I can tell. They're looking at you like you've done something wrong."

Derek chuckled. "You told them I wouldn't tell anyone?"

"I did, but they don't care," Samantha said.

"You think they're about to throw me in the Sound? Get rid of me?" He then quoted *The Godfather* to say, "He's sleeping with the fishes."

Samantha laughed. "We're not Italian, but I wouldn't put it past them. They look like older guys, but they're strong as an ox. It's all the stubbornness. It's good for the muscles."

At the Martha's Vineyard harbor, Roland and Grant walked ahead of Samantha and Derek and waved down a taxi. Together, the four of them crammed in, with Roland in the front seat and Samantha in the middle back between Derek and Uncle Grant. The taxi driver was the same one who'd taken Samantha and Derek to the retirement facility last time, and he spoke excitedly.

"I had no idea you two were still here! The married lovebirds!"

Samantha's eyes widened with panic. Roland turned to glare at her, and Samantha shook her head and smiled.

"We thought we'd stick around a little while," Samantha said. "Maybe we'll even move here."

"It's gorgeous here. When the tourists leave, the Martha's Vineyard community really comes alive. We're there for each other, you know." He grinned.

Suddenly, Roland spoke. "I don't suppose you know someone named Chuck Coleman. He's lived on Martha's Vineyard for thirty-two years."

"Chuckie! Of course I do. Oh, we've had our share of laughs, I'll tell you what. Chuck's a prominent figure around here. Well, he was before he went into the facility. I understand why he went, though. Rumor has it he struggles walking these days, which sounds exhausting. Besides that, he's a social guy. It's good he has so many friends around him all the time over at the facility. I take it that's who you're meeting today?"

Roland nodded sullenly. "That's right."

After the taxi dropped them off, the four of them hovered outside the facility. Roland and Grant looked on the edge of running back.

"You hear that guy? Saying Dad has been a prominent figure on the island?" Roland furrowed his brow with a mix of curiosity and anger.

Samantha understood, then. It was remarkable to them that Chuck had gone on to live such a wonderful secondary life, even outside Nantucket Island. It was as though they hadn't allowed themselves to consider what his life had been like at all. To them, he'd been dead.

Inside the facility, a middle-aged man with glasses greeted them kindly and said Chuck was in his room and expecting them. Roland and Grant thanked him, looking stricken. Together, Samantha, Derek, Roland, and Grant followed the employee through the hallways, past the recreational area, and finally to a private entrance that read: Chuck Coleman.

Chuck had dressed up for the occasion. He wore a button-down, a suit jacket, and a pair of slacks, and he'd gelled his hair and spritzed himself with cologne. As his sons entered the room, his eyes widened, and the corners of his lips quivered into a smile. For a long time, nobody said anything.

And then, Grandpa Chuck extended his hands, stretching his fingers toward his sons. "My boys," he said softly. "My boys are here."

Confused and emotional, Roland and Grant stepped closer and took one hand each. Samantha's throat swelled. They seemed like little boys.

It was clear the three Coleman men needed time to themselves. Samantha stepped forward and greeted her grandfather with a kiss on the cheek, then led Derek into the waiting area. Once there, they collapsed onto the stiff couch and remained quiet for a little while, both happy not to be in the midst of the men's intense conversation. *How could they overcome thirty-plus years of resentment in just an hour or two?*

"I heard from Patrick yesterday," Derek admitted. He brought an arm over Samantha's shoulder. "He said he's doing well. Sophie is in a different wing than he is, so he doesn't see her at all, but they keep in contact with letters."

Samantha dropped her head on Derek's shoulder. "Letters. Wow. That's so romantic, isn't it?"

"From what I could tell, Patrick seems really serious about getting sober this time," Derek said. "And he spoke like I've never heard him before. Apparently, Sophie and Jared never had children, but she always wanted them. And she asked Patrick what he thought about eventually starting a family. Obviously, she's in her early forties now, so time is running out for her. But she froze her eggs in her early thirties, which means there's a little more time than normal."

"Wow," Samantha murmured. "I wonder if she told Jared she froze her eggs."

"I have a hunch she didn't want to be in that relationship for the rest of her life," Derek said. "Maybe she thought, eventually, she would find a way out of it. Maybe she thought she'd eventually meet someone like Patrick."

A woman in her forties or fifties approached the front desk with a box of what looked like donuts. She was bright-eyed and smiley, and she greeted the man behind the front desk by name.

"Hi, Oriana!" the man responded. "How is your day going?"

Samantha froze with intrigue. Oriana was not the most common female name. *Was it possible Oriana was one of Chuck's daughters? Was this her aunt Oriana?*

"Just fine. I'd thought I'd pop in to see Dad and give him a treat," Oriana explained.

The man at the front desk furrowed his brow. In a voice too quiet for Samantha to hear, he spoke to Oriana and then gestured toward Samantha and Derek on the couch. Samantha couldn't breathe. Slowly, Oriana turned and gazed at them, her lips in a paper-thin line.

As Oriana closed the distance between them, Samantha jumped to her feet. Grandpa Chuck had said he didn't want the two sides of his family to meet— but maybe that wasn't up to him.

"Hi. You're Samantha Coleman?" Oriana furrowed her brow and continued to hold the box of donuts.

"And you're Oriana Coleman," Samantha said.

Oriana closed her eyes. "My goodness. I never thought this day would come." She turned to gaze back through the halls of the facility, then said, "Roland and Grant are both back there?"

"They've been in his room for about forty-five minutes," Samantha explained.

"And they haven't killed each other yet? That's a good sign," Oriana said.

Samantha sighed. "So, your dad's been pretty open with you about his past."

"He saw no reason for secrecy after everything that happened on Nantucket," Oriana explained. "He told us the story of Margaret, Roland, and Chuck when we were old enough to understand. It really hurt us that they didn't want to know us."

"That makes sense. It would have hurt me too," Samantha said.

Oriana lifted her shoulders. "I should go."

"Stay," Samantha urged.

"No. I hate to admit this, but I'm frightened of them. If I ever do meet them, it won't be today."

Samantha nodded, then rifled through her purse to find her business card. She passed it to Oriana, then said, "Let's stay in contact."

Oriana pressed the card against her chest. Her eyes filled with tears, but she blinked them away. "Thank you," she whispered. "I know how much it means to my dad that you're all here today. It has to be one of the greatest gifts of his life."

Oriana turned on her heel, placed the box of donuts on the counter, then left the facility. Samantha watched as she left. Her hair glistened and bounced as she hurried away, as though the emotional toll of meeting Samantha was too enormous.

She had a hunch that wouldn't be the last time she saw Oriana Coleman. That day, their lives changed forever.

Chapter Twenty-Five

It was the first day of July, exactly two months since Samantha had signed the divorce papers, learned of Jessabelle's death, and catapulted herself into the summer of a lifetime. Although her head spun with whiplash, her heart was full.

Despite the horrors of the solstice party, Samantha had agreed to have a smaller, family-only party that evening. *Was she insane?* She hustled around the Jessabelle House in a swimsuit top and a pair of jean shorts, sweeping and scrubbing and laughing at how crazy things were. On a ladder, Derek adjusted the last required shutter on the exterior of the Jessabelle House and chuckled at Samantha's anxiety.

"Are you okay down there?" he asked.

"It's the first time the man's coming to Nantucket Island in thirty-two years! I want everything to be perfect," Samantha shot back.

Derek descended the ladder with a smile. "I highly doubt that Chuck Coleman will take off for Martha's

Vineyard if there's a small smear on the window or one of the hors d'oeuvres doesn't taste right."

"Ugh, that reminds me. Where is Rachelle? She said she'd be here by now to start prepping," Samantha said.

Derek's strong hands caught her shoulders. As he massaged her upper back, the tension receded, and she closed her eyes. "You can't just do that," she moaned. "It's cheating."

"It's going to be a fantastic party," Derek said softly. "All eyes will be on Chuck, not on you."

Samantha winced. "I just hope it doesn't end like the last party."

"Patrick won't be here to have his nose punched, so I think we're good," Derek said.

Samantha placed her head on Derek's chest and listened to the beating of his heart. As she'd already told Derek, she'd spoken to the rehab counselor, who'd reported that both Patrick and Sophie would be released in two weeks' time. There was still no word from Jared, although she was sure he'd pop back up for a messy divorce one of these days.

Tires crept up the driveway. Samantha hurried to the far side of the veranda to see Rachelle and Darcy pop out of the car and wave. As they walked toward the house, their summer dresses whipped around their long, tan legs. Oh, to be so young. Samantha prayed they wouldn't make as many mistakes as she had. Then again, making mistakes was a part of life.

At the kitchen counter, Rachelle, Darcy, and Samantha began to prep appetizers, a main course, and dessert for later. Rachelle explained this meal would allow her to show off her skills much better than the last solstice party had, and Samantha said, "That's good. If it's awkward, we're going to need something to talk about."

Only days ago, Samantha had sat her daughters down to explain the full story of the Coleman family, including Margaret's affair, Chuck's second family, and the two million dollars that had kept Roland and Grant quiet for decades. Darcy and Rachelle had been captivated. At the mention of two million dollars, their jaws dropped. Samantha reminded them that Roland hadn't given her a cent of his money since she'd gone to school and, further, that she preferred it that way.

"I'm proud that your father and I built our lives on our own," Samantha said.

Samantha knew very little about Daniel's current state. He was probably still in his high-rise apartment with his beautiful thirty-four-year-old girlfriend, pretending he had more energy than he did. Because Derek seemed in nearly every way Samantha's "match," she marveled that she'd allowed herself to stay with Daniel for so many years. Her love for him had been poisoned, and it had nearly taken away all her self-esteem. She was so grateful she'd gotten it back.

Family members began to arrive around six. Charlie came first with his wife, Shawna, and his youngest daughter, Maria. He hugged Samantha and muttered, "I don't know everything that happened, but the stuff I do know has already blown my mind."

Samantha laughed as the hug broke. "You ready to see our grandfather again?"

Charlie shook his head, flabbergasted. "Mom said something about Jessabelle's diaries. That's how this all came to light?"

"They were hidden in the wall behind the bookcase,"

Samantha said. "When I started reading, I figured I'd just learn a thing or two about Jessabelle's many romantic flings."

"I'm assuming you also learned about those?"

"Oh yes. Jessabelle knew how to have fun." Samantha chuckled.

After that, Charlie's other children, Darren and Jordan, arrived, followed by Hilary and her daughter, Ava. Uncle Grant came next with his wife, Katrina. They hugged Samantha stiffly as though they still weren't sure what to think about her tie to Patrick and Sophie.

A moment after their arrival, Uncle Grant pulled Samantha aside and said, "I heard from Sophie today. She told me how difficult it's been with Jared for many years. I suppose Katrina and I had our suspicions about Jared, but we didn't know it had gotten so bad." He shook his head, then added, "And we had our suspicions about the drugs too. But verbalizing them broke our hearts too much, so we kept everything to ourselves. Anyway. I apologized to her. I told her I wished she would have felt comfortable coming to us for help. And I told her..." He paused, his eyes filling with tears. "I told her that when she comes home, we will help her with everything. With the divorce. With the next steps of her life. And she thanked me and told me she loved me. And I realized, as a father, that's all I ever really want to hear."

Samantha's heart shattered. She hugged her uncle, overwhelmed with bittersweet happiness. "Sophie is going to come home," she told him. "And she's going to be healthier and happier than ever."

Soon after that, Uncle Grant's other daughter, Ida, arrived with her husband, Rick. They looked shell-shocked and distrustful as they mounted the steps.

Already, almost everyone sat at the long table Samantha had set up on the veranda, sipping wine and chatting about simple things as a way to break the ice. Ida and Rick greeted Samantha and sat near Grant and Katrina. They did not smile.

Roland's car appeared at the far end of the long driveway. Together, the entire family watched as it traced the driveway's path all the way to the steps of the veranda. In the front seat were two men, with Estelle in the back. Quickly, she popped out and opened the door to the passenger side as Roland hustled around the car and removed a wheelchair. Grant stood and hurried down the veranda steps to help shift Chuck into the wheelchair, which they then carried to the veranda carefully.

The brothers placed Chuck's chair on the veranda so that he faced the entire family he'd left behind so many years ago. Suddenly, everyone stood and walked toward him. Nobody knew what to say.

"Please. Let me speak first," Grandpa Chuck began. His voice wavered nervously. "I have thought about this moment for the past thirty-two years. Never in my wildest dreams did I think it would happen. Yet here we are, together. And I really couldn't be any more pleased.

"Thirty-two years ago, I moved to Martha's Vineyard to be with my girlfriend, Mia, and my daughters, Oriana and Meghan. Much to my shame, I had these daughters while still married to Margaret. These actions worked to destroy my relationship with all of you— and I know I will never get the time back that we've lost.

"I hope you will accept an apology from a very old man. Know that I've loved you all deeply over the years. More than that, I did love Margaret so dearly." He lifted his eyes to the Jessabelle House, captivated. "This is the house where Margaret grew up. It's the house where I first met her sister and her parents so many years ago when I was just a silly kid with nothing to lose. Margaret and I had no idea what we were getting into. I suppose nobody does when they fall in love."

Beside Samantha, Derek took her hand and squeezed it. Her heart skipped a beat.

One after another, the Coleman family members stepped forward to introduce themselves and hug Chuck. The emotion took its toll on him as, very soon, his cheeks were wet with tears.

When it was finally time, Samantha ushered everyone to the dinner table, explaining that Rachelle had planned every recipe while she and Darcy had been her sous chefs. After his first bite of baked eggplant drizzled in a balsamic reduction, Grandpa Chuck closed his eyes and said, "I can't believe this. I'm eating the most scrumptious food— and my great-granddaughter, Rachelle, prepared it. This must be a dream!"

Rachelle's smile was brighter than the sun. "There's more where that came from, Great-Grandpa," she said.

"I look forward to trying all of your recipes, Rachelle," Grandpa Chuck said. "I'm ninety-one, so we had better hurry up. I hope you're ready to cook."

There beneath the dying light of the July evening, the Coleman family broke bread together for the first time in decades. Their laughter cascaded across the dunes, along the beaches, and over the waves of the strong Atlantic. Jessabelle and Margaret, sisters and best friends till the end, would have loved it. The Jessabelle House, the home of so many memories and so many days gone by seemed the perfect place to start anew.

Coming Next in the Coleman Series

Pre Order Love Runs Deep

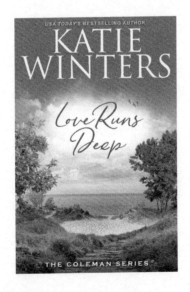

Other Books by Katie Winters

The Vineyard Sunset Series

Secrets of Mackinac Island Series

Sisters of Edgartown Series

A Katama Bay Series

A Mount Desert Island Series

A Nantucket Sunset Series

Made in the USA
Middletown, DE
21 July 2023

35544994R00126